The
Wedding
Promise

The Wedding Promise

Search for Love Series

KAREN ROSE SMITH

For women who have been abused—may they find the courage, shelter and love that they need to thrive.

Chapter One

Beth Crandall knew what she was doing even if everyone else in her life didn't believe she did.

Seated in the plastic surgeon's exam room on a mid January morning waiting for a consultation, she felt a little bit anxious. But in her thirty years she'd known a heck of a lot more fear and anxiety than this.

In the past two months, she'd seen more than a few changes in her life since she'd been reunited with her biological family. Being reunited with her sister and parents had been daunting. Moving to York, Pennsylvania, to get to really know them had been a huge adjustment for everyone. Especially for her adoptive parents.

The door suddenly swished open and a tall, broad-shouldered, lab-coated physician strode in. From her Internet search, she recognized the specialist she'd come to see, Dr. Samuel Benedict.

Her gaze went to his face and she was taken aback for a moment by his piercing blue eyes. She looked away, but not before she'd gotten a glimpse of thick black hair, a little longer than most physicians wore it, and a face that was craggily handsome.

He held out his hand and she studied it a moment before she took it. She didn't give her allegiance, trust, or friendship easily...for very good reasons.

"Beth Crandall?" he asked, making direct eye contact.

This time she didn't look away. "Yes."

His dark brows furrowed. "I'm a little confused. I have two names listed here. Present day charts from your family physician in Pittsburgh, but then a folder with old records under the name Lynn Thaddeus."

How was she going to explain this in two easy sentences?

He looked down at the name again, then he snapped his fingers. "My gosh! You're Max Thaddeus' lost daughter."

"*Found* daughter now," she said with a small smile, glad this world-renowned plastic surgeon, who traveled from country to country repairing children who had been hurt from bombs, shrapnel, or birth defects, understood at least some of her background.

"Do you know Max?" She couldn't call Max Thaddeus "Dad," even though he was her birth father. She called her adoptive father Dad. It would be all too confusing.

"Max's law firm handles foundation work for Kids Cause and some of my personal matters. He's generous with his time."

"Kids Cause," she mused. "I found you because of your work with children. It took me two months to schedule an appointment."

"My schedule is usually booked when I'm in town," he said matter-of-factly, without any arrogance.

"I was lucky. Your receptionist called me with a cancellation."

"There are many qualified plastic surgeons in York. And if you're from Pittsburgh, there are quite a few there."

"This is important, Dr. Benedict. I wanted the best, and not only the best, but a doctor who cares. If you take care of children, you care."

When he canvassed her face, she wondered if he could see that little girl inside who'd been kidnapped from her room one dark night, who'd been held captive for three months, who'd been adopted and given a chance at a normal life.

"We should talk about what you think I can do." He sounded as if she might not know what that was. But she'd researched him and researched him well.

Pushing her long brown hair aside, she ran her forefinger from the top of a scar at her temple down past her eye to below her cheek bone. "I'd like this gone."

So many doctors now stared at their computers and didn't make eye contact with their patients when they had an appointment with them. Instead of heading for the computer on the stand at the counter, Dr. Benedict pulled the stool from the built-in desk and pushed it directly in front of the end of the exam table. Then he sat on it and studied her face.

"May I?" he asked.

Of course, he wanted to examine the scar. Of course, he wanted to touch her face. That's why she was here.

"Go ahead," she said, bracing herself.

However, to her surprise she didn't need to brace herself

when his fingertips touched the top of the scar. In fact, she found herself wanting to lean into his hand.

While he ran his finger over and around the scar, he directed gently, "Tell me about how it happened. Was this a take-away from the kidnapping?"

Apparently he didn't pussyfoot around a subject, he stomped right into it. But then he was a busy surgeon.

"No, not from the kidnapping. I was only three when I was taken." She stopped, but then went on with, "I don't remember much from those three years. More is coming back as I spend time with Amanda, Max, and my sister Clare. I seem to remember Clare more than my biological parents."

"You were close," Dr. Benedict suggested as if he understood.

"I guess. I felt a bond with her right away. Maybe it's because we look alike."

He nodded, and as she breathed in, she smelled a citrusy aftershave that was altogether appealing. Was she attracted to this man? She almost felt an inner awakening, a part of her coming alive that had been dead for as long as she could remember.

"Are your memories clear *after* the kidnapping?"

"Is this part of our consultation or your curiosity?"

He leaned back and his hand dropped. "I'm trying to get to the bottom of where and when you got the scar, and why you want it to disappear. Plastic surgery isn't just about a surface fix. I want to be certain that a procedure is necessary, and if it's what you really want. It won't be covered by insurance. It's not a medical necessity."

"Max is paying for it," she said honestly.

"He feels guilty for not being able to find you all those years?"

"He and Amanda feel guilty about a lot of things. But they never could have found me. My kidnapper changed my name from Lynnie to Beth. That's the name I gave the police when they found me abandoned at a mall. Because of a lisp I couldn't even say my last name clearly. I gave my name as Beth Saddees. That's what went on my records."

She stopped for a breath, uncomfortable with repeating it all over again.

"You've had to tell the story a lot," he guessed.

"I had no memory of my early childhood, or what happened after the kidnapping, until I saw a television interview with Max, Amanda, Clare, and Clare's daughter Shara. They'd been thrown into the spotlight because Shara had run away."

"And Max was shot," Dr. Benedict noted, obviously remembering.

"I guess you were in the country then."

"I was."

"What's it like, helping children as you do when you travel? It must be so rewarding."

"Helping anyone recover from trauma or a physical impairment is rewarding. Your intake form lists your occupation as a website designer. Do you enjoy that?"

He must have realized she needed a reprieve from giving him personal information. "I do. It's a challenge to fashion a website that's unique to each client."

He studied her carefully once more, from the light brown bangs over her brows, to her white Oxford shirt, to the conservative navy slacks. "So let's get back to your scar."

Sure, they had to. He had other patients to see. "When I was a teenager, I had a best friend."

He waited for her to go on.

"Hannah had moved around a lot. Her mom was a single mom who had health problems. Hannah ended up in a group home and came to my school when she was thirteen, after her mom died. She was a firecracker—all rebellion and attitude. I was shy and didn't make friends easily."

"But somehow the two of you connected?" he guessed.

"I was being bullied. Hannah stepped in and confronted the mean girls. We became a team."

The doctor nodded as if he understood. "You were kidnapped, and abandoned, and had no connection to anyone in the place where you landed at first. My guess is that you withdrew inward. You tried to pretend if no one was out there, then no one was."

No one had ever pinpointed it so well, not even her therapist.

"Yes. I still do withdraw to some extent. But Hannah taught me to stand up for myself."

"And what did *you* teach *her*?" His eyes said he knew their relationship had been reciprocal.

"I think I taught her how to hope. When she came home with me for dinner or an overnight, she could see there were good people in the world—my adoptive parents."

Nodding to her scar, he asked again, "So what happened?"

"Hannah hated the group home. The facility housed

boys *and* girls. She felt she always had to be on guard. She didn't really have friends there. When I visited her there, my radar was always on alert."

"Radar?"

She shrugged. "From as far back as I can remember, when I would be around a new person, I'd decide whether they were safe for me to be around...or not."

"An instinct you learned when you were kidnapped."

"I suppose. Many of the kids at the group home weren't safe to be around. Especially the boys. I could tell by the way they looked at Hannah...the way they looked at *me*."

"Why did you go there?"

"Because my parents didn't approve of Hannah. I could tell. She cut class a lot. She got detention. But they didn't understand her like I did. She was my best friend." Beth's voice caught when she said it.

Dr. Benedict waited for her to go on.

"It was late winter. I visited her and it was stuffy inside the group home. We went out back. It was getting dark and we didn't see the two boys who were smoking. They started with catcalls. We tried to go back inside but one of them held the door shut. The other pressed me against the wall and tried to kiss me. Hannah jumped him but he pulled out a knife. He came at me and she stepped between us. But he was flailing with the knife and it cut my face. She was fighting off both of them when someone inside saw what was going on."

When she stopped to take a few breaths, Dr. Benedict studied her face. "Take your time."

Beth squared her shoulders and raised her chin. "I was clinging to Hannah—I didn't want her to get hurt like I had—when someone pulled me away. I was taken to the emergency department and I never saw Hannah again."

"Why?"

"The authorities transferred her to another group home somewhere else in the state. When I asked my parents to find out where she was, no one would tell them. They'd just say she was moved for her own safety."

Dr. Benedict's jaw set, his mouth tightened, and the nerve along the side of his cheek worked.

"Hannah saved my life that night."

"Have you ever looked for Hannah?"

"I've taken it as far as I can on my own—Google searches, Internet data bases. In time, that home was closed. But I've been thinking about pursuing another avenue. Amanda has a friend who searches for missing persons. She helped find Max's granddaughter Shara when she ran away in October."

"You want all the loose ends tied up and finding Hannah would do that."

"That's one way of putting it."

"And you want the scar gone because you think that will help you move on."

"Yes."

"Do you want the scar gone to make you feel different when you look in the mirror?"

"You mean to look prettier? No, that's not my reason for wanting surgery. Pretty is about so much more than a scar on my face."

"This is about inner healing."

"It is. So will you do it for me?"

His gaze met hers and when it did, neither of them seemed able to look away. However, he slid his stool back, stood, and went over to the counter where the computer was located. He tapped on a few keys, brought up a grid, then turned back to her.

"We can do an EKG and blood work today. I can schedule you for next Thursday. Will that work for you?"

It would work. The sooner she had this done, the sooner she could move on.

As Beth pulled into the parking lot at the bridal shop, she was fifteen minutes late. She'd thought she'd left plenty of time for the consultation and the drive over here, but she hadn't counted on the blood work and the EKG. She hoped Clare and Amanda and Shara wouldn't be upset. At this point she still didn't know exactly what reactions to expect from the Thaddeus family.

In a sudden flashback, she recalled her first reunion with them at her sister Clare's house.

"What should I call you?" Clare Thaddeus asked. "Lynnie or Beth?"

"I've been Beth for as long as I can remember and I'm used to it."

"Beth, it is." Clare stepped back so Beth could step inside her house.

The autumn day was crisp with the nip of a colder night to come. As Beth entered Clare's house, she focused on the open windows and the breeze instead of the three other people in the room. After a live TV interview the Thaddeus family had done because of wanting to help runaway girls like their own granddaughter Shara, Beth had recognized her sister Clare because they looked so much alike. A few memories had flooded back and she'd telephoned the TV station. That call had led to a DNA test and a reunion a week later. Her DNA said she was part of the Thaddeus family.

The woman, Amanda, with the strawberry-blond hair rose from the sofa as if she couldn't sit there a moment longer. "Lynnie," she whispered in a choked voice.

Beth had spoken with Amanda Thaddeus on the phone the day her DNA results had come in. This was her birth mother. This was the woman who had loved her the first three years of her life.

When Amanda's arms surrounded Beth, held tight and wouldn't let go, Beth felt as if she'd come home. Yet, in a way, she felt guilty about that.

Soon another arm surrounded her, a strong male arm. Tears blurring her vision, she looked up to Max Thaddeus, her father. In that moment, she remembered him lifting her high in his arms to the sound of her own giggles. Where had these memories hidden for so long?

They'd hidden in a shadowed kidnapping she barely remembered. They'd hidden in abandonment and night-mares, loneliness and fear and in an adoption that had helped her heal many wounds.

As her niece, Clare's daughter, embraced her, too, Beth realized her deepest healing could finally begin.

Entering the bridal shop now, she considered why she'd only confided in Clare about the appointment with Dr. Benedict. The other members of the Thaddeus, as well as Crandall family, knew she was thinking about plastic surgery. But they'd all told her she should do what she felt was best. Having so many people curious and knowing what was going on in her life just seemed odd. Her adoptive parents had always been overprotective and cared tons about her every minute of every day. She'd rarely let anyone else in. Now with the Thaddeus family forming a web around her, she felt unsettled to say the least.

Still, since surgery had been scheduled, she was ready to put part two of her plan in motion—finding Hannah. For this, she'd have to talk to Amanda.

Amanda, her birth mother. Amanda, who was once more marrying her ex-husband Max—Beth's birth father—after over twenty years apart.

Bev's Bridals had been a house at one time. The largest room on the first floor held bridesmaid dresses. Smaller rooms showcased accessories including bridal veils, shoes, and purses. Another room beckoned to the mothers of the bride and groom. Clare had told Beth exactly where to go—upstairs to the bridal gown collection.

At the top of the stairs, Beth stopped and listened. She could hear Clare's rich laughter. She walked into the room and spotted Clare and her daughter Shara, who'd recently turned seventeen, seated on pale blue, velvet-covered chairs facing a dais surrounded by mirrors. Shara's pregnancy wasn't showing yet.

As soon as Clare saw Beth, she said, "You're just in time. Mom wouldn't let us go back with her. She's chosen three gowns and we have to pick out the one we like."

Beth breathed a sigh of relief. "She should pick out the one she likes the best."

Shara rolled her eyes, a habit with her. "That's what I told her. But Gram has this terrible flaw. She wants to please everybody."

Beth had to smile at that. Amanda Thaddeus had been through heart-wrenching times—the kidnapping, a divorce, alienation from Clare, the scare when her granddaughter had run away. Recently, Shara's unexpected pregnancy. After Shara had run away in October, Max and Amanda Thaddeus had found each other again. So Amanda had moved back in with Max. Recently, they'd bought a house not far from her antique store, *Yesteryear's Treasures*. Amanda was decorating the house, hoping everything would be perfect by the time she and Max were actually remarried in two months. She'd offered Beth the apartment above *Yesteryear* to live in.

Beth touched the scar on her face. What would her face look like in two months? Would that be enough time for healing? Or would it look worse than it did now? She'd have to talk to Amanda about it. After all, she didn't have to be in the wedding party. Yet another part of her knew that Amanda expected her to be in the wedding party. She wanted her daughter back, and she saw this wedding as symbolic in so many ways. Beth didn't want to disappoint her, yet she had to find herself in this new family equation too.

When Beth took the chair beside Clare, Clare whispered to her, "How did it go?"

Nothing got by Shara. "How did what go?"

Just then, however, Amanda appeared in the small hall that led into the room. With a tremulous smile, she beamed at the three of them and stepped up on the dais.

"Wow," Beth said, meaning it.

Her mom was still an attractive woman with a great figure. Since reuniting with Max, she'd had her strawberry-blond hair restyled into a shorter swingy cut. Now, in ivory satin with a sweetheart neck, a cinched in waist, and ankle-length hem, she looked like a bride rather than a mother or a grandmother.

"It's beautiful," Clare murmured.

"It's elegant," Beth added.

But Shara wrinkled her nose. "It's too simple."

Amanda's face fell. "Too simple?"

"Gram. You want Gramps' eyes to pop out, don't you? I mean you look pretty and all, but you need some kind of knock-him-over factor. Try the next one."

Clare gave her daughter a look that said maybe she shouldn't be quite so expressive.

Amanda took a look at herself in the three-sided mirror. "Maybe she's right. I'll try the next one."

The next one, however, fashioned completely of Alencon lace, Shara poo-pooed too. "You look like a grandmother in that one. That high neck. Those cuffs. No, Gram, that's not it."

Clare said to Shara, "Let's try to be positive about this."

"I'll be positive when I see one I really like."

Beth had to laugh. "You said you taught her to say what she thinks. She's saying it."

Clare shook her head. "I don't think I want to bring her along if *I* pick out a dress."

"You and Joe won't pick out a date, so who knows when that's going to happen," Shara muttered.

Beth had heard the story about how Clare and Joe Lansing had become more than next door neighbors. Clare and Joe had grown closer when he'd supported her during her worry over Shara when she'd run away. After Shara had come home, though, Clare had wanted to be certain that Joe knew what he was taking on if he got involved with her. Shara's baby in this family mix complicated their situation. Clare was determined to see her daughter through having a baby, even if that meant she'd be taking over some of the parenting. So she and Joe had been dating and were serious, but weren't moving forward too fast. Beth wasn't sure what she thought about that. If they were truly in love and wanted to be together, maybe they should be, no matter what.

Unbidden, Dr. Samuel Benedict's face appeared in her thoughts. There hadn't been a ring on his finger. She wondered if he was involved with anyone. Silly for her to wonder, really. Wasn't it?

As she focused on wedding dresses once more, she realized maybe it was true that the third time was the charm. When Amanda emerged from the hall again and stepped onto the dais, they all stared wide-eyed. The dress had a forties glamour draping to it, from the shoulders to the waist, and from the waist to the hem. It was ivory satin with tiny seed pearls and sequins edging each drape. It was glamorous and bride-like and made Amanda glow.

"That's the one," Shara declared.

Clare nodded while Beth said, "You'll knock Max over in that one. You'll look so glamorous."

Amanda had tears in her eyes as she faced them. "I'm so glad I asked you to come with me."

"No veil," Clare said. "Maybe a 40's style hat. That dress needs to stand on its own."

"Maybe a headband design," Beth suggested.

Amanda came down the two steps and slipped her arm around Beth's waist. "This moment means so much to me."

Amanda had been saying that ever since Beth had been reunited with her.

"On to the bridesmaid dresses," Clare said. "This could take a while.

They'd done it, Beth thought an hour and a half later. They'd all agreed. They'd chosen off the rack dresses, just as Amanda had, so alterations could be completed in plenty of time. When Amanda and Max had finally settled on a date, there had been no stopping them. Both were determined people who knew exactly what they wanted.

As Amanda continued to tell Shara how beautiful she'd look in a mint green maternity-style, Clare whispered to Beth, "So tell me about your appointment."

"Surgery is next Thursday."

"So soon?" Clare looked surprised.

"Dr. Benedict had an opening. I'm a little worried about telling Amanda. I don't know how I'll look for the wedding."

"She won't care if you have two heads. You know that."

"I'm going to talk to her after you and Shara leave. There's something else I need to discuss with her too."

"I told Joe I'd make dinner tonight, so I do have to get going." Clare squeezed Beth's hand. "Everything will be fine. You'll see."

Beth wasn't so sure about that, but she'd like to believe it.

After Shara and Clare had left, and Amanda had put her checkbook back in her purse, Beth asked her, "Can we go somewhere for coffee? I need to talk to you."

Amanda nodded, her expression somber. "Sure. Let's go to that little family restaurant across the street."

Beth wasn't sure how this conversation was going to go. But it would be just another step in getting to know Amanda Thaddeus.

Chapter Two

Ten minutes later, Beth and Amanda were seated across from each other in a booth, coffee in front of them. Amanda looked concerned. "What's going on, honey?"

"I saw a plastic surgeon today. Samuel Benedict. He knows Max."

"Your scar," Amanda said, glancing at it, then glancing away.

"Yes. I like Dr. Benedict. He has an opening next week, so I'm going to let him fix me. But I'm a little worried about the wedding. I don't know how the scar will look by then."

Amanda covered Beth's hands with hers. "Do you think I care about that?"

"It's your special day. I don't want anything to mess it up."

"The only thing that would mess it up would be if you weren't there."

Beth let out a sigh of relief.

"Are you sure you want to do this?" Amanda asked.

"Yes. I talked with the doctor in length about it. He understands. He's a very...compassionate man."

Amanda studied her face. "I didn't realize you had an appointment with Sam. There are several plastic surgeons in that practice. Your father knows Sam well."

"He's highly involved with a foundation for kids— Kids Cause. Apparently Max does legal work for it," Beth recalled.

"Yes, he does. Sam has told us about his travels all over the world, setting up clinics to help repair children who have been harmed." Amanda took a sip of her coffee, then assured Beth, "I'll clear my schedule for next Thursday so I can be with you. Is this an outpatient procedure?"

Beth nodded, "Yes, it is. I haven't told my mom yet."

"Irene will probably want to be here. She's welcome to stay with Max and me if she wants to come for an overnight visit. I should have the house pretty much in order by then."

"Thank you. I'll let her know."

Beth turned her coffee cup on its saucer. It was always a little strange when her adopted parents and Max and Amanda got together, which they'd done a few times since Beth had come to York. They were trying to be one big, extended family. Would they ever be? Only time would tell.

"There was something else I wanted to talk to you about."

"Anything," Amanda said, her sincerity telling Beth she meant it.

At that first reunion, Max and Amanda had filled Beth in on what they knew about her kidnapper, Luther Brown, who was on death row. Beth had filled them in on her history, including her friendship with Hannah. "I want to find someone—Hannah Miller. Remember I told you about her? She was my best friend when I was in high school."

"I remember. She protected you."

Beth nodded, pleased Amanda remembered. "I've tried to find her every way I know how. It's just a no-go. You and Clare and Shara speak so highly of Gillian Bradley. I wondered if she'd help me. Tell me again how you found her and how you knew she was reputable. After all, most people wouldn't consult a psychic."

Amanda leaned forward as if she needed to be closer to Beth. "We looked for you for so long. We never wanted to give up. I was always searching for anything that might help...anyone who could help."

"Because you'd lost faith in the police?"

"Maybe. But I researched missing children cases everywhere, and a few years ago I came upon a blog. Gillian was Gillian Moore then. She hadn't been married yet. She'd helped the police find a missing child up in the hills near L.A. News media got hold of it and the story and background was publicized across the country. She'd been struck by lightning when she was a child, and after that happened, she just had this gift. She moved from the Midwest to L.A. to escape it, but there's no escaping something like that. After she moved to L.A., she found love. Nathan Bradley enlisted her help when his ex-wife took his daughters out of the country. Gillian helped find them."

"Yet she couldn't help find me."

"No. There was some kind of block there. You were one of the one per cent of the cases she couldn't help."

Might the reason have been because her kidnapper had changed her name and messed with her identity?

"She has a partner who's a P.I.," Beth remembered.

"That's right—Jake Donovan. He does the nitty-gritty behind the scenes work. When Shara was missing, he helped track down the guy she met on the Internet who'd lured her to Albuquerque. But then Gillian honed in on exactly where she was. It was amazing really. When Max and I met with her in New Mexico, I'd taken along Shara's jewelry. Gillian received sensory perceptions from it."

"So you trust her."

"Implicitly. She and Jake set up a foundation that helps funding for their travel and that kind of thing. They charge on a sliding scale according to their client's ability to pay. But mostly it's a pay-it-forward situation. Everyone they help wants to pay back, so they donate to the foundation."

"Do you think she'd help me?"

"I can give you her number. Or, if you can wait until the wedding, she's supposed to fly in for it. You could meet her and then decide if you want her help."

Beth liked that idea. She liked it a lot. "That sounds like a plan." She hesitated. "There's something else."

"You know I'm here to listen." Amanda was trying to make up for all of those years when she *couldn't* listen.

"I need you to talk to Max about something for me."

"What?"

"He's insisting on paying for my surgery. Dr. Benedict said it's not a medical necessity so insurance won't cover it."

"We expected that."

"I don't want Max to pay for all of it. I need to pay for some of it."

"But, Beth—"

"Seriously, Amanda. I need to be an active part of finding a new life, of getting out into the world when I've always been afraid to. I make good money as a web designer. I want to pay him back, little by little, even if it's only a nominal amount each month. He's already said he won't accept it, but that's why I want you to talk to him. Please."

Amanda studied her. "He's a stubborn man."

Beth smiled. "I've noticed that."

"But I'll talk to him for you. I'll explain how important it is."

"I'd appreciate that." Beth hesitated again and then she asked, "Do you know anything about Dr. Benedict? About him personally, I mean."

"Not much. I've only ever spoken to him about his work."

"I read articles about him online before I made my appointment. I just wondered since Max knows him—"

"What exactly do you want to know?"

Beth felt herself blushing. "Never mind."

"Beth, what?"

"I just wondered if he's married...engaged...that kind of thing."

Amanda's smile was knowing. "So you're interested."

"I didn't say that."

"You didn't have to. But he could be a lost cause. From what I understand, his work's his life. I don't know why. I never heard the story behind why he does what he does. But he's out of the country at least half of the year."

"I see."

Amanda squeezed Beth's arm. "You need to find someone more eligible."

No, Beth thought. *My life is complicated enough right now.* She really didn't need a man in it. Not any man at all.

Clare put the finishing touches on a simple but hardy meal, the kind that Joe liked—roasted pork chops, baked potatoes, and green beans.

In the kitchen with her, Joe glanced at it all approvingly. "I wish Shara would change her mind and eat with us."

A landscape architect, Joe worked with his dad at their nursery and he had muscles that proved it. An Afghanistan veteran, he was square-jawed and hand-some. A little zip of male-woman awareness zinged through Clare whenever she looked at him.

She felt that zip now as she said, "Shara says she has a lot of school work and she'll get something later. I don't know how to treat her anymore, Joe. She's seventeen and pregnant, trying to establish independence and I'm trying to let her. The father of her baby wants to sign away his parental rights and that could be for the best. She seems to have accepted the fact Brad never had feelings for her. She's giving more attention to these on-line classes than I've ever seen her give to regular school work, but I think she feels isolated."

After Joe sat at the table and she sat across from him, he said, "She wanted to do computer school instead of going to the high school. That has cut her off from kids her age. But she has us and your mom and dad."

"She doesn't have friends like she used to. They're not pregnant and she is and most don't want to associate with her." Clare sighed. "But I think she enjoyed today and helping Mom choose a gown. She was a big help."

"See any gowns *you* like?" Joe asked with a wiggle of his brow.

"Joe..."

"When you say my name like that, you think I'm going to back off the subject, but I'm not. We have to come to decisions of our own."

On Christmas Eve, Joe had asked her to marry him. He'd been so sweet and romantic about it. But she had postponed giving him an answer for several reasons— their lives were in such turmoil with Shara's pregnancy, she was re-establishing sisterly bonds with Beth, and she was getting used to the idea that her mom and dad were getting back together again.

"Don't give me the same old excuses," he said. "If you have to postpone your decision, give me *new* excuses."

It was hard to tell if he was joking or serious.

Finally, she gave him her bottom line excuse. "How can I make a decision about us when I don't know how much responsibility I'll have for Shara's baby?"

"We could adopt Shara's baby, then we'd know exactly what kind of responsibility we'd have."

She put down her fork and stared at him. "You'd really want that?"

"Wouldn't you?"

"I don't know. Besides, don't men want their *own* children?"

"You should know I'm not like that. This child would be ours if we adopted it."

"I can't do that to Shara."

"She might want you to."

"In the short run, perhaps, but in the long run I think she'd have so many regrets I don't even know if we could still be mother and daughter."

"Someone's going to have to make a decision soon," Joe insisted. "I know Shara's only seventeen, but at some point she has to take responsibility for her life, if not her child."

Clare knew he was right. But, still, so much had happened in such a short amount of time.

"What does your sister think?" Joe asked.

"She's going through her own adjustments. She's having surgery on Thursday to fix the scar on her face."

"Really? That was sudden."

"It's elective surgery. Insurance doesn't cover it. The doctor knows my dad. I think she said he had a cancellation."

"The scar's not that noticeable."

"To us, it isn't. But I think Beth believes by removing it, she can remove part of her past life."

"If only it were that easy."

Losing her appetite with the seriousness of their discussion, Clare studied Joe. Scars from Afghanistan were still with *him* in more than physical ways.

He spent a few minutes digging into his food, but then he returned to their previous subject. "When *are* we going to get married, Clare?"

She just couldn't think about marriage right now. "Can we at least wait until after Mom and Dad's wedding to talk about this again?"

"In March?" He poured more gravy on his potatoes. "As I told you before, Clare, I'm a patient man. I can wait until March. But then no more excuses about Shara or your sister or your parents. Got it?"

Clare had never been married. Having her own child out of wedlock and seeing her parents' marriage fall apart hadn't led her in that direction. So she supposed now she was just running scared. She looked across the table at Joe, a man who had been patient and kind and honorable during trying times.

"I promise you in March we'll make decisions."

He looked satisfied with that. But at this moment, Clare couldn't exactly say what any of those decisions would be.

Chapter Three

"I promise no matter what life throws at us, I will never lose you again. I'll stand beside you and hold onto you, love you, and cherish you for as long as I live."

Beth sat in the first pew of the Pine Hill church that was decorated with white spider mums, listening to her birth parents renew their vows. She was getting lost in the heartfelt wedding promise in Max's voice. Her father's voice. He was more than Max but less than Dad. She already had a dad who she guessed would be so hurt if she called someone else that.

At the altar, Amanda, who she couldn't yet think of as a *mom*, held onto Max's hands. "I will trust you and support you and never let go. I promise to respect you and cherish you and trust you every day of my life."

Max and Amanda had written their own vows and Beth understood now why they'd wanted to. Their words were heart-felt. After everything they'd been through, Beth believed that they truly meant what they were promising each other.

She wished she could stop feeling guilty that she had somehow broken up and torn up their marriage and the family. In a way she had, or rather her kidnapping had. Fortunate not to remember much, the professionals called her lack of memory "traumatic amnesia." However, amnesia didn't prevent the emotions from swirling inside of her since her reunion with her birth family. Those emotions were one of the reasons she'd decided to move to York and work through all of this. Though, in spite of everything, in spite of their separation for years, she did feel close to Clare and, in a real way, to Shara too.

Clare, who was sitting beside her, had tears running down her cheeks. Beth leaned close to her. "This is a happy occasion, you know."

Clare smiled wanly. "I know. I'm just so happy for them I could burst. It's been such a long hard road for all of us." She looked aghast. "For you too. I didn't mean it wasn't hard for you too."

"I understood exactly what you meant. I told you before, Clare, you don't have to watch every word with me."

As they returned their attention to the front of the church, Beth touched her face where her scar had been. Her surgery had been successful. Although a slight red line still remained, Dr. Benedict had assured her it would fade altogether if she stayed out of the sun for a few months and used sunscreen after that. She'd spotted him among the assembled guests when she'd walked down the aisle. Would he say "hello" at the reception?

Beth focused on Max and Amanda as they exchanged rings and the minister as he gave a final blessing. Amanda looked beautiful in the gown she'd chosen, and Max looked totally distinguished in his tux. Joe and a friend of Max's who'd flown in from Texas sat across the aisle on the groom's side. Beth saw Joe wink at Clare when she looked his way. Clare blushed like a teenager and Beth hoped their relationship would work out. But Shara and her baby came first to Clare, and Beth wasn't sure how Joe fit into all of that. She wasn't sure Clare knew, either.

At the end of the ceremony, Clare and Beth preceded Amanda down the aisle, escorted by Joe and Max's best man—Frank Grey, who was a lawyer like Max. Beth spotted Dr. Benedict again and felt her heart flutter a bit. He'd done his magic. He'd been so kind, so caring, so…sexy. She *never* thought in those terms. Her therapist, who had tried everything from age regression to self-hypnosis to the deepest meditation with her, believed she had been abused by her kidnapper and had turned off anything to do with male-female relationships...and with sex. Her subconscious was telling her it was so much easier to live without the complications of romantic involvement with a man.

Yet, now something about Samuel Benedict had awakened feelings she wasn't sure she'd ever had at all. Would he *stay* for the reception or would he have to leave right after the ceremony? After all, he *was* a busy surgeon.

Lost in thoughts that disconcerted her, she almost stopped when she spotted the woman on the bride's side of the church. She was a pretty woman with light brown hair and a hundred-watt smile. Having seen a photo of Gillian Bradley online—some of the cases she'd helped with had gained her publicity, most of it unwanted—Beth recognized the psychic who had found Shara. Gillian didn't like to be called a psychic, but her gift for finding missing persons, especially missing children, was documented. Beth had hoped to talk to her *before* the wedding, but Gillian had called Amanda, explaining she was dealing with a last-minute emergency in California. A police department had needed her help, and it had been hard for her to say no. Nevertheless, the foundation she worked for had somehow managed to get her on a private plane to fly in this morning.

Beth needed to talk to her. She had to put together this puzzle that was her life. Once she could see the big picture, then maybe she'd have peace. Maybe the knot that had lived in her chest all her life would finally unwind. Maybe she could break out of the cocoon she'd woven around herself.

The receiving line seemed to take forever. Not only did the guests want to congratulate Amanda and Max, but they wanted to hug Beth too. Most of them called her Lynn or Lynnie. She knew they saw her as that little girl they'd once known or heard about. But she was so removed from that little girl.

Except when she was with Clare, her sister. Then a few memories surfaced—Clare holding her hand, Clare and she whispering back and forth in a secret language, she and Clare stealing a sticky bun from the cooling rack after Amanda had baked them.

As the last person left the receiving line and passed into the adjacent social hall, Clare asked her, "Are you all right? That had to be tough."

"It wasn't so bad. Everyone means well."

"Did you remember any of them?"

Amanda's friend, Natalie, seemed to jiggle a memory loose. "The woman whose name was Natalie Barlow. I imagined this vague picture of her carrying boxes into a house."

"You saw a picture?"

"I imagined it...or the memory came back...or something."

"You imagined it right. She helped us move into the house you were taken from. She and Mom have been best friends for years." Pausing, then changing the subject, Clare said, "I saw Gillian arrived in time for the wedding. When are you going to talk to her?"

"As soon as I can."

Beth couldn't take her eyes off of her mother and father. She could think of them that way because she'd never called her adoptive parents that. They'd always been Mom and Dad. There was something a little distant about "Mother and Father," and that's the way she felt about Amanda and Max. They felt like distant family. She hoped that would change but she didn't know when or how.

The wedding cake was beautiful, all white flowers with real mums surrounding each layer. When Amanda and Max cut it, they gazed into each other's eyes and the love between them was so obvious. They'd promised their lives to each other all over again. A wedding promise. Would she see how that really worked out? Or would she want to go back to her life in Pittsburgh, a life that was protected, safe, even boring at times. Her adoptive parents had been invited to this celebration but declined. They didn't want Beth to feel uncomfortable or to take any attention away from the bride and groom.

When the music began playing for the first dance, Joe danced with Clare, of course. Beth awkwardly danced with Max's friend, Frank. One song segued into the next and other couples joined them on the dance floor. She wasn't sure how she could politely and tactfully go back to her seat. Dancing with a man her parents' age made her...uneasy. Remnants from a time she didn't remember?

She was about to trip over her own feet on purpose, or something like that, when suddenly she was released from Frank's arms. Dr. Benedict was standing beside them—so tall, so exceptionally handsome in a dark suit and royal blue tie that made his eyes even bluer.

He asked the man loosely holding her, "May I cut in?"

Max's friend smiled and released her. To Beth's surprise, when Dr. Benedict took her into his arms, she wasn't uneasy at all.

Now that was just so weird.

"Hi," he said, and she had to smile.

"Hi, back. Did you enjoy the ceremony?"

"It's great to see Max happy. And Amanda, too, of course."

Beth nodded, not knowing where to take the conversation from there. But she didn't have to worry because he handled it. "You looked uncomfortable dancing. I thought I could...rescue you."

"Do you do a lot of that?" she joked.

"In my line of work, at times I do."

"Thank you," she said.

"For rescuing you?"

"For making my scar practically disappear."

"It will disappear—*outwardly*."

She knew exactly what he meant, but she didn't want to deal with the subject on healing inner scars right now. "I'm not your patient any more," she said, warding off advice he might want to give.

"No, you're *not* my patient. That's why I asked you to dance."

Their gazes locked, and Beth became mesmerized by what she saw in his eyes. There were moments in Beth's life that she remembered vividly—when Hannah had saved her from certain harm, the day she went to live with her mom and dad, her high school graduation. But this was one of those moments too.

"I have a request," the doctor said.

Was he going to ask her out on a date?

"I've checked out the websites you've designed, and I like them."

Her websites? What did they have to do with this? Disappointment cut through her that this wasn't a personal conversation. Yet, somehow, no matter what they talked about, in this man's arms, it felt personal. She'd never taken dancing lessons but somehow she was following him perfectly.

"Are you taking on clients?" he asked.

"Of course." Her voice became more polite now, rather than friendly. "That's how I make a living."

"With your skill, I thought you might be booked up and too busy to take on a new project."

"That depends on what it is, or who the client is."

He thought about that, then said, "I'd like you to redesign the website for Kids Cause. It would mean starting from scratch. I met with the director and the board, and we all believe it would be beneficial to have more than a main page with an explanation of what we do. We want to incorporate social media feeds."

"I can do that," she assured him.

"Do you *want* to do it?"

She wasn't exactly sure what he was getting at. In the next moment, he made himself clear.

"Everyone who works for Kids Cause has a passion for what we do. We'd pay you your hourly rate, of course. But we'd also like you to put your heart into this site because *our* hearts are in it."

She thought about children who needed care and the doctors who would do that for free, funded by the foundation. She'd checked out the present website. She'd Googled Kids Cause and read everything she could find about them. She'd even Googled Dr. Samuel Benedict. But everything she'd discovered about him had concerned his professional practice and his cause.

"I can put my heart into designing your website, but I have a condition."

His eyebrows arched. She was so aware of the fabric of his suit under her fingertips, the scent of his aftershave, the lines around his eyes either from sun or hardship. She didn't know which.

"I want to do it for free."

"Beth," he said chidingly.

"Dr. Benedict," she said just as chidingly.

"Call me Sam," he insisted.

She knew if she did, she would be taking a step toward a different relationship with him. "All right, Sam. But that's my condition."

"Can you stop by my office so we can consult about it, maybe Monday? I'm free from eight to nine."

"I can be there."

He tightened his hand around hers a little. "Now that that's taken care of, let's just enjoy the music."

Beth felt decidedly off-balance after Sam returned her to her table...after he said, "I'll see you on Monday."

Clare nudged her elbow. "You look good together."

Beth could feel her cheeks reddening. "He wants me to design a website."

"A new client and a new romantic prospect?"

"I don't know if I'm ready for a romantic prospect, and I don't know if he's on the hunt for one."

"There's Gillian," Clare said, pointing to the woman who had a gift not many people could understand.

"Do you think it's okay if I just pull her aside?"

"It's what she does, Beth. She'll understand. She's here because she cares about our family. Go talk to her."

As Beth approached her, Gillian smiled and said, "It was a beautiful wedding."

"Yes, it was," Beth agreed quickly. "Can I talk to you for a few minutes?"

"Sure, you can. I was just trying to mingle."

"It's hard to join in someplace where you don't know very many people, but then I guess you're used to doing that."

"I do it a lot. Where would you like to go to talk?"

"Let's try the bride's dressing room. No one else will be there and I'd like to do this in private."

Gillian's gaze questioned her, but she didn't say anything or ask questions. She simply followed Beth down a short hall into the room where Amanda had dressed for her wedding. The room was in disarray. After all, four women had dressed in there.

Beth swept clothes off of two chairs, quickly fixed them on hangers, and positioned them on a door apparatus that had been hung for that purpose. Gillian had already taken a seat, and now Beth took the chair across from her. "I'd like you to find someone for me."

Gillian cocked her head and waited.

"She was my best friend in high school. She saved my life."

"Have you tried finding her before?"

"I've Googled her name, Hannah Miller. But if she was adopted or she married, there might have been a name change. I haven't come up with anything."

Gillian nodded as if that weren't unusual. "Do you have anything of hers...any kind of remembrance? A necklace, an earring, a shoe string?"

Beth thought about the last night she'd seen Hannah. She'd been wearing that over-sized red coat. There was something about that coat...

But that memory was lost in murky shadows of recollections she couldn't retrieve. Post traumatic stress did that—with a kidnapping...and with an attack.

"No, I don't have any remembrances."

"That's going to make this harder, at least on my part."

"The name of the group home where she lived when I knew her was Pennsylvania Partners in Pittsburgh. She was transferred from there to another group home in the state."

"I'll put my partner Jake on the group home and her name."

"Do you need to know anything else?"

"Not right now. Your memory gives the best clues we have. So let's wait until Jake gets the ground work done, then we'll shake up those memories and see if I can sense anything from them. Is that okay with you?"

Truthfully, she didn't know if it was okay with her. Just what kind of Pandora's Box might she be opening?

Chapter Four

Beth was nervous. Not the sweating, *turn-around-and-go-home* nervous. Rather an *I-wonder-what's-going-to-happen* kind of nervous. Sam shared his offices with two other plastic surgeons. She realized using his first name came easily and that was because of the dance they'd shared. It had been almost intimate. How could that be when all those people were surrounding them and watching them? But it *had* been intimate, especially when Sam had pulled her a little closer after they'd stopped talking.

She tried to shake pictures of the wedding from her thoughts as she entered the reception area. Max and Amanda had left on their honeymoon, one they richly deserved. They should be on a beach in Curacao right now, concentrating on each other.

Over the years they'd had to concentrate on so much else. Her kidnapping had taken all of the air out of their marriage. Her kidnapping had made Clare feel unloved, unwanted, and unappreciated. Even at the age of five and the years going forward, her sister had known she was in second place because finding Lynnie was all that had mattered to her parents. Year after year, when it had become obvious her sister might not be found, her mother and father's emotions and their attempt to hide them had broken their family apart. Clare had acted out, becoming pregnant, having Shara. Although Amanda and Max had been there for her, they'd been apart—a single mom and a single dad. It wasn't until Shara had run away in the fall that they'd come together again. It wasn't until Beth had seen their interview on a national TV show that her own life had changed.

Memories were funny. They popped up unexpectedly like helium balloons that had been pressed under water for years. Beth had seen Clare's face when she was being interviewed and she'd known she was her sister. Max and Amanda might not seem like parents yet to Beth, but Clare was definitely her sister.

Considering the wedding again, the promises Max and Amanda had made to each other echoed in her mind. Wedding promises had meant something to them years ago and meant something to them again. Her adoptive parents' wedding promises had meant something too. They were usually a happy couple. She was causing them grief now because of her exploration into her biological family, but she hoped...

She hoped what? That the Thaddeus family and the Crandall family could be one big happy family? That could be a pipe dream, just as much of a pipe dream as she herself walking down the aisle someday. Her scar was gone now, but she was damaged goods. How could she ever expect a man to deal with that?

There were several patients in the waiting area and Beth went to the receptionist's window. A different receptionist sat there than the one who had greeted her on past visits.

When the woman looked up, Beth said, "I'm here to see Dr. Benedict."

"Your name?" the woman asked. Her tag said her name was Rhonda.

"Beth Crandall."

Rhonda smiled. "Ah, yes, the website designer. I guess I won't need to see your insurance card." She motioned to the door at one side of the reception room. "Come on back."

Beth went through the door, remembering her first visit here. She had to say she was more nervous now. That was because she was stepping into uncharted territory.

She reminded herself she wasn't. She should just treat this like a business consultation.

Rhonda called to her, "Just keep going until you reach the end of the hall. Dr. Benedict's office will be directly in front of you. I'll buzz him that you're on your way."

As Beth walked down the hall, an LPN passed her. She was so intent on where she was going that she forgot to smile. When she realized that, she stopped. She'd had a lot of therapy, years of it, and she considered herself normal now, as normal as a person could be who'd once been kidnapped. But she also knew when she didn't pay attention to her surroundings and the people around her, that was cause for concern. It meant she was drawing inward. She did that when she was worried or nervous or uncertain about the future. Having control and a plan were ways that she coped. She had no plan for today.

Sam's door was partially open. When she peered inside, he smiled and beckoned to her. "Right on time. I have about an hour to give this. Do you think it's enough?"

"We can always follow up with a second consultation, or shoot e-mails back and forth. I rarely do meetings like this in person."

Sam gave her an odd look then motioned to the maroon leather club chair in front of his desk. "Have a seat and tell me why you don't do face to face meetings."

"I find them...distracting," she said honestly. "When I e-mail back and forth with a client, we stick to content. We don't get caught up in incidentals quite as much."

"In other words, you don't have to worry about getting to know a person when you don't meet in person."

Just as she'd realized before in her time spent with him, Sam was very perceptive. "I get to know my clients through what they ask me to do. Once in a while we get a little chatty in between projects."

"I suspect you're not as chatty as your clients."

She met his gaze directly. "This is a consultation about the website you want me to design, not about my personality."

"Touché," he said with a grimace. "I'm sorry if I offended you. But you intrigue me."

"Because I was kidnapped?" she asked bluntly.

"No, Beth, not because you were kidnapped. I see lots of trauma of all kinds, from auto accident victims to burn victims to grenade and IED explosion victims to limb damage. I try to repair it. Yet no matter what I repair physically, I can't undo the emotional harm. I'm simply intrigued by you, your attractive appearance, your intelligence, your survivor attitude."

All of that caught her off-guard. And as far as her being attractive—she was wearing a white Oxford blouse and navy slacks, her usual business uniform. How could he find that attractive?

"Hmm," he said. "I've made you speechless. That's not a good thing, and I'm not usually quite so forthcoming. But that's one of the reasons you intrigue me. You seem to call for being forthright."

After a long moment when neither of them looked away, Beth reached for her messenger bag and the electronic tablet she kept inside. She removed it, opened it, and hooked up to the network in the offices. She was glad to see they'd put in free Wi-Fi on her first visit. All doctors should do that because of the waiting time.

Then she became business-oriented. "Tell me what you want to accomplish with this website."

He understood their time to discuss the project was short. "Greater visibility, of course. We have a fund raiser coming up and I'd like you to spotlight that. I have jpegs of our logos, background information, and that type of thing on this." He took a thumb drive from his desk drawer and held it out to her.

She leaned forward and reached for it. Their fingers brushed and she felt those tiny tingles of excitement scampering around inside of her again. This wasn't the time or place for them. She dropped the thumb drive into her purse.

"Do you have a color scheme you want me to use?"

"I hadn't thought about that," he confessed.

"Red, white, and black would probably be the most effective and striking. But any photos we use would give a softer, friendlier feel."

"There are photos on our present website of the places the doctors have worked, some of the children we've helped, and brief profiles of doctors on upcoming tours. We post a schedule as we plan the year."

She nodded. "You said you're interested in social media. I can set up feeds for Branches, Facebook and Twitter. Would you like a blog forum also?"

And so it went until they were five minutes short of an hour.

Beth's phone played *Eye of the Tiger*. Sam's brows arched and she shrugged.

"You should take it if it's important," he suggested.

She checked her screen. "It's Amanda," she murmured.

"Amanda and Max are on their honeymoon, aren't they?" Sam asked.

"They're supposed to be. I hope nothing's wrong." She lifted the phone to her ear, feeling comfortable taking the call in Sam's presence because he knew the couple.

"Hi, Amanda. Is everything all right?" She realized, although she didn't feel super close to Amanda and Max yet, she cared about them and cared about them very much.

"Nothing's wrong," Amanda responded. "We're having a wonderful time. I just forgot to tell you something.

That antique armoire you liked so much from the 1950s came in the day before the wedding. The movers put it in the back room. With getting ready for dinner and then the wedding itself, I forgot all about it. Maybe you could ask Joe and he could find someone to help move it up to your bedroom."

"It can wait."

"For another ten days?" Amanda asked. "Seriously, Beth. You have a key to my shop. Make the armoire yours."

"I hate to bother Joe."

"He's going to be family soon. He doesn't mind, believe me. Do you want me to call him?"

"No, I don't. You're on your honeymoon. You shouldn't be thinking about armoires."

Amanda laughed. "You know my mind goes a mile a minute. Besides, I need something to do while Max gets his Weather Channel fix."

This time Beth laughed. "All right. I'll call Joe later and see what he says. Have a wonderful time."

"I love you, Beth," Amanda said, and there was just the slightest hesitation before Beth's name. Beth knew Amanda wanted to call her Lynnie. But there was no going back. There was no erasing the years that she'd thought of herself as Beth.

She also couldn't say "I love you" back. The words just wouldn't come. However, Amanda seemed to understand that because she ended with, "I'll see you in about ten days," and then clicked off.

"A problem?" Sam asked.

"Not really," Beth answered truthfully. "I'm still getting settled in the apartment above Amanda's antique shop."

"*Yesteryear's Treasures*," Sam said.

"You know it?"

"Pine Hill isn't that big and it's not that far from York. Her shop is one of the best antique stores around."

"And you like antiques?" Beth asked, surprised.

"You're looking at me as if I just grew two noses. I can't say I like antiques per se, but I do like rustic. I guess the house decorator would call my place 'masculine rustic'."

"You have a house?"

"No, a condo. That way I don't have to worry about maintenance when I'm gone."

Gone. That's right. He traveled a whole lot, to chase his profession...or for other reasons. She was curious as to what those were.

"So Amanda called from her honeymoon because she was thinking of you?"

Beth smiled. "In a way. She'd showed me this photo of an armoire that was coming in, and I really liked it. It's the 1950's waterfall design. It just has so much character, and it fits in with the orange oak bed I found at the thrift store. I'm still paying rent on my apartment in Pittsburgh, so I didn't want to splurge here in case this didn't work out. Amanda took her bedroom suite for her spare bedroom in their new house but she left the rest. Staying above Amanda's antique shop seemed the perfect solution. That way I wouldn't be barging in on them or Clare, and I'd be independent."

"You don't feel a bit spooked staying there all alone? With the antique shop underneath you?"

"You mean at night? Remember, I've had lots of therapy. We put my PTSD demons to rest a long time ago."

Though she had had a nightmare the first night she'd slept alone in that apartment. That was just strange-apartment blues. That really hadn't meant anything. Still if she had to admit the truth to herself, she never felt completely safe. Vigilance was part of her makeup. Her therapist had warned her that that might never change.

"Are you seeing a counselor now?"

She could tell him that was a question that was too personal, but somehow she wanted to answer it. "I hadn't seen Linda for years. But we had a session after I realized the Thaddeus family was my birth family. We talked about the information they gave me about the kidnapping. I haven't spoken with her since I moved here. I can call her if I need her. Pittsburgh is only a drive away."

"So you've learned to roll with the punches?"

"Doesn't everyone have to learn that eventually?"

"I suppose. So what are you going to do about the armoire?"

"Amanda suggested I ask Joe to move it, and maybe he'd know someone who could help."

"I could help."

"You move furniture in your spare time?" she teased.

"You'd be surprised what I've had to move on my stints overseas. Sometimes we have to dig latrines, set up camp, construct buildings. We think we're going into a sterile situation and we're not."

"So *you've* learned to roll with the punches."

"Much of the time."

She had a feeling there was a story there. Everyone had a story. Although Sam seemed friendly and interested in her, she sensed he had his guard up, too. Because of his profession? Because attachments were difficult because of it? Because of past history?

Sam took a business card from the holder on his desk, wrote something on it, and then extended his hand to her.

She took the card without touching his fingers. She knew better this time. "What's this for?" she asked.

"If you need help moving the armoire, call me. If I'm free, I'd be glad to help."

"Do you want to help because you're a friend of Max's?" She had to get to the bottom of this. She had to know if this doctor was interested in *her*, which seemed like such a far-fetched possibility.

"Max is a friend and he's out of town. You're his daughter—his long lost daughter. He saw us dancing at the reception, and when we talked, he asked me to look out for you while he was gone."

Her shoulders squared and her chin went up. "I don't need anybody to look out for me."

Sam rubbed his hand down his face. "I obviously shouldn't have told you that. But there *is* another reason I'm giving you my number."

She waited.

"I like you, and I think you might like me…just a little."

"I've heard doctors have enormous egos," she said with a straight face.

He burst out laughing. "I've heard that, too, but you can't believe everything you hear, can you?"

She slid his card into her purse, along with her electronic tablet. "If we need your help, I'll call."

He stood, came around the desk, and lounged against the front of it. He was less than a foot away. His charcoal suit was impeccably cut, his white shirt didn't have a wrinkle, his silver and red striped tie lay exactly as it should.

Trying to ignore his proximity, she explained, "I'm hoping to finish up with a client's website this evening. I'll have time to fit yours in over the next few days. Will you be doing all the approvals, or will we have to consult with someone else?"

"The board trusts me to handle this. They delegated, so you'll just be dealing with me...except for final approval by the board's director."

That idea made her heart quiver a little. "I'll e-mail you a link to a temporary hosting spot where you can check out what I do. I should send that to you by Wednesday. I don't expect to run into any problems, but you never know."

"I appreciate your following up so quickly."

When she stood, her thighs practically brushed his knees. She was farther away than when they'd been dancing. Somehow, she felt closer. She'd never been this close to a man in just this way before.

"You have a fund raiser looming," she reminded him. "If you want donations rolling in, we have to get this done. I'm hoping to accomplish that by the end of the week."

"A woman with a purpose."

"I always have a purpose."

Right now, her purpose was to get out of his office...get out of the building...and just breathe.

On Wednesday evening, Sam didn't know what he was doing at *Yesteryear's Treasures*, standing before the shop's door ready to knock. He'd seen Beth Crandall two days ago. He'd received the link to a temporary hosting site around noon. He hadn't expected to hear from her until she'd completed the website. But she'd called this evening just as he'd gotten home to his condo—at a decent hour for a change. He'd considered ordering take-out since his refrigerator was empty, but...

Her voice had been hesitant. "You're probably busy, but you said to call if Joe needed help."

If Joe needed help, not if *she* needed help. Sam had considered his answer before he'd responded. "I just got in. Are you moving it now?"

"Joe has time and we'd like to. The steps are a little steep."

"I can be there in ten minutes if the traffic isn't too bad."

"Sounds good. Thank you."

"No thanks necessary. See you soon."

This was definitely going to get personal, he thought now. And maybe complicated. But Beth did intrigue him. On Monday the offer to help had just come out of his mouth in a blurt. Afterward he'd considered the fact that he'd made a mistake.

Beth wasn't the type of woman a man had a fling with for a weekend. Not that he was into flings, but he wasn't into serious commitment either. How could he be with his professional commitments? Professional and personal would definitely clash.

Still, Beth was beautiful when that vulnerability entered her eyes, and even when it didn't. When it did, he just wanted to put his arms around her and hold her close. That was a first. When he was attracted to a woman, he usually had something else in mind.

But maybe that's why he was here. Beth was an enigma, and he was curious about her.

When Beth opened the door, most of the thoughts in his head fled. She wore her hair tied back, her bangs dipping over her brow. She didn't wear makeup. In jeans and a T-shirt that proclaimed *Yesteryear's Treasures* on it, she looked like the proverbial girl next door. Yet she was beautiful and a puzzle he'd like to figure out.

"Come in," she said, motioning him inside.

In spite of what he'd said, he did know something about antiques. The plank flooring, the desks and tables and armoires that gave off the scent of polish, yet a little bit of the musky decades-old scent too, drew him inside. The bell over the door had tinkled when Beth had opened it. But as he looked around, he spotted a security panel and surmised the store had a state of the art alarm system.

He noticed an office to the back of the store on the left, a small space. A hutch held a computer and there were file cabinets and a set of bookshelves. On the right, there was a closed door. A storeroom maybe?

"Joe will be here any minute," Beth said. "The armoire's back here."

He had been right about the storeroom. Beth opened a door and they stepped inside. The first thing his eyes fell on were stairs.

"They lead up to my spare bedroom," she informed him as she followed his line of vision.

Sam's gaze fell on an armoire that was at least seven feet tall and four feet wide which was positioned near a rear exit door. Drawers lined one side with pulls that were intricately scrolled yet sturdy. The left side of the armoire was one long door, and he guessed coats would fit inside.

"Do you mind?" he said as he reached for the door.

Beth shook her head and he opened it to the smell of cedar. "This is nice."

When he'd opened the door, he'd moved a little closer to Beth as he had in his office. He caught the faint scent of flowers. Although her wardrobe was usually tailored, he sensed a woman underneath all that who liked to hide.

Did she even know that's what she was doing?

Suddenly the front door to *Yesteryear's Treasures* flew open and a man called, "Beth?"

"Back here," she called.

Joe Lansing strode to the back of the store. Sam had met him on Saturday at the wedding. It wasn't hard to see that he and Clare were involved. Beth had told him Joe had been a member of the Army reserve, and had done a stint in Afghanistan.

The man's hazel eyes now studied Sam. "It's good to see you again," he said.

"I hope I can provide the muscle you need," Sam answered.

Joe looked from Beth to Sam as if he were wondering if it was just muscle Sam was providing. Not only women could be intuitive.

"Let's get to it then," Joe said. "Clare convinced Shara to help her with dinner, but they each have their own opinion of how to do things. I don't know how that's going to work out when there's a baby in the house."

Beth mostly stayed out of the way as Joe and Sam carried the armoire up the back steps to her bedroom. There was plenty of room on the wall where she'd decided to place it. Once they'd pushed it to the perfect spot, she said, "Thank you so much. I think this piece of furniture is really going to start making this feel like my home."

"If you stay in or near York, the Thaddeus family will be ecstatic, you know that. But how will the Crandalls feel?" Joe asked.

"I don't know," she admitted. "And I don't want to hurt Mom and Dad. I can do my work wherever I am. I might split my time between Pittsburgh and here. I'm just not sure what's going to happen yet, Joe. You know how that is."

"I certainly do. I can't even get Clare to agree to an engagement. If you have any influence—"

Beth held up her hands in a stop gesture. "Oh, no. You're going to have to do your own persuading. Clare's got a mind of her own. All of my convincing in the world won't change what she thinks."

"Life changes and big decisions don't always go together," Sam offered.

Joe studied him again. "I never thought of it that way. With the baby coming, maybe Clare's afraid to make any big decisions." He said to Beth, "I'll see myself out. I'll bet you want to start filling that thing up."

Beth laughed. "I might have to go shopping to do that."

"I'm sure Shara and Clare would love to give you a hand. Take care and I'll talk to you soon."

Both she and Sam heard the door to the kitchen close. She realized she was at home, in her bedroom, with a man she hardly knew. But he'd done her a favor and she couldn't just let that pass. "I could order a pizza. In thanks for your help," she added quickly.

Sam shoved his hands into his back pockets and studied her. "I can leave if you're not comfortable with having me here."

"Let's go into the living room," she said softly, thinking that might make a difference.

She motioned to her couch in a nubby blue and green material that was comfortable to sit on. Once they were seated on it, they might as well have still been standing in her bedroom. She was totally aware of this man in a way she hadn't been aware of a man before. She suspected the crinkle lines around his eyes hadn't just come from laughter. The wave of his black hair told her that if he let it grow even longer, it would wave more. His polo shirt and jeans spoke of a good quality, not a discount store. So did his sneakers. If *she* was intriguing to *him*, *he* was intriguing to *her*. But she wasn't sure she wanted him to know that...yet.

"I haven't been around men much on a personal level," she confessed. "Yes, for business, I deal with everybody. My adoptive dad and I are close. But I was an only child and didn't have male relatives. And I just never wanted to...keep company with men."

"That's an old-fashioned term, but it fits. So you're saying you didn't date in high school or college?"

"Maybe I felt self-conscious because of my scar. Maybe it was because of other reasons. But I didn't date in high school, and I didn't go to college. I took on-line courses for web design. I had a knack for it so it just developed."

"You're not anti-social. I watched you at the wedding reception. You can talk to anybody."

"Wanting to and feeling comfortable about doing it are two different things. I like alone time. I like quiet time. I'm not a party girl."

He smiled. Changing the topic, he said, "Joe is taking on a lot, getting involved with Clare now."

"He knows that, and she knows that. I think that's why she's not making any commitments. But if she doesn't make one soon, she could lose him."

"The baby will take up much of her time and attention."

"It will. But Amanda is going to help. In fact, she's thinking of selling *Yesteryear's Treasures* and babysitting for Shara full time. I hate to see her close the store when it's something she loves."

"Max told me she opened it after their divorce. Maybe it was something she needed then, and maybe she doesn't need it now. Purpose in life changes."

Sam was in his early forties and she wondered if his purpose had ever changed. "When did you decide you wanted to become a doctor?"

Shadows seemed to pass over Sam's face, and he became very serious. "I knew from a young age. I knew children needed to be heard and fixed when they could be."

She was sitting about six inches from Sam, yet it didn't really seem that far away, especially when he stretched his arm along the back of the sofa. It was near her shoulder...near her hair...near her face. He leaned toward her. She leaned toward him. She held her breath because the look in his eyes possibly meant he was going to kiss her.

However, before he could, her cell phone played. She was so tempted to let it go to voicemail. But what if it was her mom in Pittsburgh?

"Go ahead and take it," Sam said, his voice husky. "I don't mind."

When Beth pulled her phone from her purse, she saw Gillian's number rather than her mom's.

"I do have to take this," she said. "It's the person who's trying to find my best friend."

"You hired a private investigator?"

She wasn't sure if she wanted the truth to slip out so Sam would leave, or so he would stay. But she said, "No. I didn't hire a private investigator. Gillian Bradley is a psychic."

Chapter Five

As Beth answered her phone, she watched Sam's expression. At first there was none. That was his "doctor's face" as he calculated, analyzed, and decided how he was going to react. Maybe he'd have that down until she was finished with her conversation with Gillian.

"Do you have news for me?" Beth asked.

"I'm afraid not. Jake couldn't make headway with the group home...not yet anyway. So he's searching state by state, starting with Pennsylvania but then branching out. If Hannah's name was changed with an adoption, or it was further changed with a marriage, it's going to take some time. I just wanted you to know he's on it."

"And what about you?" Beth asked, feeling a boldness she didn't usually feel. But this was her life. This had been her best friend she was trying to find. It was time to do that. She could just feel it, though she didn't know exactly why.

"I'm going to be tied up for the next week or so. I'm working on a missing person's case here with the police.

Nathan and I have a parent-teacher conference with Matthew's teacher, and…" She paused. "I want to give Jake the amount of time he needs to work on this before we start probing into your memories. The thing is, Beth, when we start digging around in your memories, it isn't only memories of Hannah that might pop up. And I'd like your therapist on-call, or else we could meet in person with her. That's why I'm calling. I want you to think about all this and decide what would be best for you. I know you want to find Hannah, but you might also find another part of yourself, maybe even Lynnie. Is there a reason you've been patient about this for all these years, but now you're suddenly *impatient*?"

Gillian had the nicest way of getting to the heart of the situation. Amanda had told Beth that, and now she could see it firsthand. "I'm not sure why I feel this pressure right now. That's the only thing I can call it. Maybe because my life has taken a different direction?"

"Or, maybe you're still connected to Hannah in a way that's rising up again. I don't question these things, Beth. There's a reason why you're at this point in your life, and you're talking to me."

"So I should just keep open to what I'm thinking and feeling and let you and Jake work."

"Exactly. And consider everything we've talked about."

"Okay, I will."

"It wouldn't hurt to talk about this with someone you trust, other than your therapist, I mean."

"Maybe Clare," Beth responded.

"Possibly. Or else someone who isn't quite as close to the situation."

Instinctively Beth's gaze sought Sam's. She still couldn't read his expression though he looked concerned. She'd see how he reacted to the idea that she was talking to a psychic.

After an exchange of good-byes, Beth cut off her cellular connection to Gillian.

As Beth sat on the sofa, about the same distance from Sam as she'd been before, she took a quick sideways glance at him.

He was watching her. "That sounded serious."

"It was."

The silence between them continued until, looking a bit baffled, he said, "I don't quite know what to say. I don't know whether to ask you about the psychic or butt out of your personal affairs."

"I guess that depends on whether or not you want to be involved in them," Beth said honestly.

He looked away toward the window and the maples beyond. "What if I told you I wanted to know more about this?"

"I'd have to ask why."

"Partly out of curiosity."

That disappointed her. Then he went on. "But I also don't want you to be taken advantage of."

"By a fake psychic? Believe me, Gillian's the real deal."

"How do you know that?"

"I know that because she has a ninety-nine per cent success rate in finding missing persons. I know that because Amanda vetted her when she was trying to find me. Gillian couldn't find me, and we don't know why that was. Maybe because the man who took me messed with my identity so much that I didn't know who I was. He named each little girl he took after the daughters in *Little Women*. He assigned each of us a role."

"Do you remember this?"

"I...uh..." A picture flashed in her mind.

"Beth?"

"I'm not sure. I learned his name and about the journal he kept when I connected with the Thaddeus family. Yet at this moment, I also remember pretty little dresses with pinafores." She said it distastefully because the words left a terrible taste in her mouth.

"You can see the dresses?" Sam asked.

"Vividly." She could remember a red one with a white apron and a blue flowered one with a navy pinafore. "I can *see* them. I never did before. I guess this is what Gillian meant."

"I don't understand."

"She was just telling me that suddenly I seem to be in a hurry to search for Hannah, and that I have to remember I might unlock memories in my past that I haven't had access to up until now. If she and I meet, she thinks it might be a good idea if my therapist is there."

"It sounds as if this Gillian is responsible."

"She's more than responsible, Sam. She finds lost children. She found a man's high school sweetheart. She found Shara."

"I thought Amanda and Max found Shara through some lead in her e-mail."

"That lead took them to New Mexico. Gillian met them there. She's the one who found Shara through her jewelry."

When Sam was silent, Beth knew that maybe he needed just a little more proof that Gillian's capabilities, whatever anyone called them, were true. "Gillian met her husband because he was searching for his daughters. His ex-wife had taken them out of the country, only he didn't know that at the time. Gillian led him to them. She and her partner don't get paid per se. They work for a nonprofit foundation that's basically funded by the people they help. They're never short of donations, and that's because they do good work."

Sam's body language was a little different now, not quite so rigid, definitely more relaxed. "You've intrigued me. Now I want to meet her."

"She was at Amanda and Max's wedding. That's when I spoke with her for the first time in person."

"Where does she live?"

"California, near L.A. Her husband owns a company which specializes in computer security. He's very down to earth from what Amanda says, and a devoted dad."

A shadow seemed to pass across Sam's face and she wondered what that was about...and if it had something to do with becoming a dad.

"Tell me what you think it means to be a devoted dad," Sam suggested.

"Actions matter. My adoptive dad spent a lot of time with me. I was wary of men. But my dad didn't let that faze him. He made sure he was there at family dinners every night. He made sure he stopped in at my room to have a private conversation and find out about my day. He never missed a school event. Everything he did, he did for me and my mom—from working to planting a tree in the front yard. That's devotion. Gillian's husband has two daughters from a previous marriage. He admits he wasn't the kind of father he should have been when they were married. But after his divorce, he began appreciating his daughters so much more, and that's why he had to find them. He wanted custody of them. Now he and his ex share custody, and they work on putting the girls first. Matthew is his and Gillian's, and from the very beginning, Nathan has gotten up at night, baby sat, did anything a mom would do. He takes over when Gillian has to go out of town. They work as a team. That's devotion on both their parts."

Studying Sam, she asked, "What does being a devoted dad mean to *you*? Have you ever tried it?"

"I shouldn't have started this," he muttered.

"But you did."

"It was a mistake. Maybe this whole conversation is a mistake."

"Were you going to kiss me before the phone rang?" she asked bluntly.

"Yes, I believe I was. But that probably would have been a mistake too. You have a lot going on. I have a lot going on."

"You mean the fund raiser."

"Yes, and another trip at the beginning of May. I'm supposed to be in Africa for a month. Maybe longer."

"I see." Beth said the words but she wasn't sure she did see. Sam Benedict had been doing this for years, and it wasn't just "get out of med school, get into a practice, and find a crusade" enthusiasm. It seemed to be much more.

"Do you plan to keep traveling?" she asked.

"I don't have a reason *not* to travel. It's my work, Beth."

"You're a doctor, a plastic surgeon. There's all kinds of work you can do. Why travel to foreign countries? Because it takes you away from here?"

Sam seemed to go a little paler. He seemed to withdraw. "What are you insinuating?"

"I'm not insinuating anything. I'm trying to find out if there's a reason you don't want to plant roots, have a family, and stay in one place."

"You're poking too much."

"I see. You're curious so you ask questions. I'm curious but that's considered poking."

"I think I'd better go."

Without a kiss. Without the connection she'd felt before. Without a good reason why he didn't want to share.

Her problem was, maybe she'd shared too easily. But he'd seemed so kind, compassionate and interested.

She really didn't have a clue about men—what they wanted, what they felt, what they dreamed, what they hoped. If they didn't know how to communicate, well, she was at a total loss.

Sam stood to leave. She was trying to think of a way to get back on an easier footing when she heard the clump, clump, clump of footsteps on her wooden staircase outside. The footfalls were emphatic and there was a bump every so often.

Of course, Sam heard it too. "Are you expecting someone?"

"Not unless Amanda came home from her honeymoon early and wants her old apartment back."

"They made promises, Beth."

"Yes, they did, but promises can be broken as they found out once before."

"That could make them both even more determined to make these last."

Did Sam Benedict believe in promises that lasted? Was she willing to take the risk to find out? Or had he had enough personal conversation tonight, and that meant he wouldn't be pursuing any more? That wouldn't surprise her either. She'd learned long ago there were very few people she could count on, and she didn't know Sam well enough one way or another to put him in any category...though she'd been hopeful they could at least become friends.

Suddenly the kitchen door flew open and Beth's adoptive mom, Irene Crandall, burst in.

"Mom, what are you doing here?"

Her mother was short and plump with fly-away brown curls which she tried to keep tied in a ponytail. She insisted on wearing big hoop earrings when she wasn't working and either dark pink lipstick...or dark red, depending on her ensemble. Today she was wearing a grass-green suit and wedge heels. Her cheeks were red from the exertion of climbing the stairs and dragging her suitcase behind her.

"I came because I miss you and I wanted a visit. If you're going to move to York, then you're going to have me as an apartment guest."

"I have a spare bedroom, but it only has a single bed. Can you be comfortable in that?"

"For a night or two."

"I have to work."

"All the time?"

"Not nights, and I can probably get away for lunches. Did you bring your knitting?"

"I did."

"Good. While I work on websites, you can knit."

Although Irene didn't know who Sam was, she said, "You can't talk to her while she works, you know. It distracts her. She has to focus, she says."

Sam smiled, and she could see her mother was already enamored with that smile.

"Mom, meet Sam Benedict. He's the doctor who performed my plastic surgery."

Although her mom had driven here for her surgery, she'd missed meeting Sam. She and Amanda had spent time together while Beth had been in recovery. She hadn't noticed tension between them when she'd awakened and they'd brought her home. They were both trying.

"Am I interrupting something important?" her mom asked. "Another consultation? Your scar's almost gone."

"This wasn't a consultation," Sam said. "I'm not her doctor anymore, and we've become friends."

So he'd admitted to the "friend" word. Interesting.

Her mother looked from her to Sam, and then said, "I see."

Beth wasn't sure what she saw. There wasn't anything to see.

"It was nice to meet you, Mrs. Crandall," Sam said. "I'd better be going. I know you have a lot to talk about."

Sam's tone seemed to ask, *Beth, does she know you're consulting a psychic?* She still wasn't exactly sure what he thought about it.

"Mom, just sit on the couch and relax. I'll get us tea after I walk Sam to the door."

Her mom seemed to take her advice.

At the kitchen door, Sam asked, "Are you comfortable with your mom here?"

"Sure, I am. She just wants to make sure she's not missing any part of my life. I actually appreciate that. I just don't know what to do with it sometimes."

He smiled. "I'm glad you can appreciate it. Many women would think she was prying."

"I'm not many women."

"I'm finding that out."

She wasn't sure if he was pleased by that, or put off by it.

"I'm on track with the website design," she assured him. "I'll e-mail you tomorrow, and we can go back and forth with what you might want to change."

He checked the living room where her mother had found the remote and turned on the TV. "Are you sure you're going to get any work done?"

"I will. I'll get up early and let her sleep late. It's amazing what I can get done if I get up at sunrise."

"So you're an early riser too."

He didn't say it, but it was something else that they obviously had in common.

Then with a wave and a good-bye, he was gone.

As she heard his footfalls on the steps, she wondered if commonalities were enough to start a relationship...or if feelings mattered more. She imagined that feelings might trump all.

When Beth returned to the living room, her mother switched off the remote and looked up. "So what's going on with him?"

"I don't know what you mean."

"Oh, yes, you do. You were standing close to him and you don't like to stand close to men. He was looking at you as if...well...he was looking at you with that look men get when they have something sexy on their mind."

"Mom!"

"You're my daughter. I know you. What's going on?"

"I like him. I liked him as a doctor, and I like him as a man. We danced at Amanda and Max's wedding reception."

"Do you know anything about him?"

"I know he's Max's friend, and he does a lot of work for kids, most of it out of the country."

"Isn't *that* interesting? I guess it doesn't give him much time for a personal life."

Sometimes Beth thought her mom wasn't perceptive at all, and then other times, like this, she realized she underestimated her. Irene Crandall had been a caring nurse who'd become a stay-at-home mom to love Beth to bits before returning to a part-time nursing schedule. She was protective—sometimes too protective. Nevertheless, there was something she had in common with Amanda—she seemed to understand relationships.

Because of that, Beth asked, "When you and Dad got married, did you believe it was going to last forever?'

"We didn't just *believe* it was going to be forever, we

were *determined* to make it last forever. A good marriage doesn't happen because two people are in love, or in lust, or whatever. It happens because they're committed."

"Max and Amanda were committed." She felt a little guilty talking about this with her mom, but sometimes she had to get it out with someone.

"As much as I wish sometimes that I didn't like Max and Amanda Thaddeus, as much as I wish sometimes *you* didn't like them, I can't judge them. Having a child kidnapped, not knowing what happened to her... I can't even imagine how that would impact a relationship. But the important thing seems to be they found their wedding promise again."

Their wedding promise. Yes, they *had* found it again.

To change the subject, Beth asked, "Would you *like* a cup of tea?"

"Or hot chocolate?"

"Did you eat?"

Her mom waved that suggestion away for the time being. "I can make an omelet or something after you tell me what you want to talk about. I believe there's something."

There was that mother's intuition again. "I started a search for Hannah."

Her mother was silent for a long heartbeat, then she asked, "What brought this on?"

"I've wanted to do it for a long time, and now I just feel compelled to do it."

"Compelled?"

"Like Hannah needs me to find her. I know it's crazy, but that's how I feel."

Her mother sighed. "Then it's not crazy. Where are you going to start?"

"I'm going to start with a private investigator and his partner Gillian who Amanda used when she searched for me, and again when she found her granddaughter."

"Are they expensive?"

"They do this work on a sliding scale that pays their expenses. Their foundation is funded by donations, and Max said he'd donate if I need his help."

At that, her mother's mouth thinned into a narrow line. "You know we'd help too."

"Thank you. I appreciate that. But let's see what happens first. I might be coming back to Pittsburgh soon. Gillian thinks I might need my therapist present if we delve into the past."

"Oh, Beth."

"Mom, I believe it's finally necessary. There's so much I don't remember, and maybe I never will. But there are also memories there that could help."

Her mother got a far-away look in her eyes. But then she asked, "And how does this woman think she's going to be able to help you find Hannah? What's so special about her?"

"She's a psychic."

Her mom's eyes widened. Her mouth rounded. Her face even flushed a little. "You'd better give me a double dose of hot chocolate because I think I'm going to need it."

Chapter Six

Although Sam was scheduled with back-to-back appointments all day Thursday, he and Beth still managed to e-mail back and forth about a half-dozen times concerning the website.

Late Friday morning Beth sent him an e-mail that it was finished, and he should take another look. He did and was totally pleased with the result. He also realized their business association was at an end, and he didn't like that thought at all. Ever since Wednesday evening he'd been trying to forget about her in a personal sense. After all, did he want to be associated with someone who believed a psychic could solve her problem? Did a psychic who wasn't a fraud actually exist?

On the other hand, he couldn't forget the sway of Beth's hair around her face, the way her eyes lit up when she challenged him, the vulnerability she tried to hide yet was always there. For some reason, she made him feel vulnerable, too, and he didn't like that at all. Still, he usually faced feeling uncomfortable to get to the source.

How else could a man solve a problem?

Though Beth wasn't exactly a problem. Was she?

Good question. He took out his phone. E-mails were impersonal. This was personal. He texted her. **Have lunch with me?**

Her reply wasn't instantaneous, and so he wondered if he should have done this at all. But soon a return text asked, **Why?**

That question was so in character with the woman he was coming to know. **Because I want to talk**, he tapped in.

About the website?

That brought a smile to his face. Because even though she hadn't used an emoji, she was joking with him.

About life in general. How about the Corner Cafe? They have great ribs on Fridays.

What time? she texted back.

He'd be free after one so he texted. **One-thirty?**

She texted back, **I'll meet you there.**

However since this wasn't a business meeting, he responded, **I'll pick you up.**

After a few beats, as he tapped his foot rather vigorously, her text came in. **I'll be ready.**

When he picked her up, she was. He didn't even make it up the deck stairs above *Yesteryear's Treasures* before she was out the door and joining him on the landing. She was wearing hunter green slacks today with a pale green blouse, a no-nonsense leather jacket on top of all that. A gold clip held her hair back over her right temple. She wore no jewelry, but he thought he did detect just a slight sheen of lip gloss.

After she followed him to his car, he opened the door for her.

"Max and my father do that," she said.

He frowned. "What category does that put me in?"

"Chivalrous," she said with a smile.

He'd been afraid she was going to say "older." After all, he was a decade older than she was. Why was he even thinking about that? They were just going to have lunch and talk.

After he switched on the ignition, he asked, "Is your mom still here?"

"No, she left yesterday. The apartment's small. I needed to work. She could only do so much cooking for the two of us, or shopping, for that matter. If Amanda had been here, maybe the two of them would have had lunch. I don't know. The whole situation's a little weird."

"Are you handling it okay?"

"For the time being. But at some point I'm going to have to decide whether to stay here or go back to Pittsburgh."

"And you're worried that either way you'll disappoint someone."

"Yes, and it's hard for me sometimes to keep in mind I have to do what's best for me."

"Why is that so hard?"

"My therapist says—"

"Beth, what do *you* say?" He cut her a quick glance. He knew that if she relied on what her therapist said, that would be a cop out. She wouldn't be getting to the heart of the matter *or* tapping into her emotions.

After sending him an annoyed glance, she fastened her seatbelt. "*I* say—that I tried to please everybody all my life so I didn't get into trouble. I tried to fly under the radar. If no one knew me, or they didn't see me, then they couldn't hurt me."

Well, he'd asked for it. "That makes sense, and I imagine that it's hard to grow out of that point of view."

He knew all too well about not making waves so as not to get hurt...about not making waves so somebody he cared about didn't get hurt. Maybe he and Beth were more alike than they both knew. He'd taken care of *his* situation by getting his mother to the hospital, by telling the authorities what his father had done, by testifying to make sure he never did it again. Right. But he always had the feeling his mother had resented him for it even though he'd done what was best for her own good as well as his. Losing a father had been a small price to pay when that father was a deadbeat and an abuser of women and kids. He'd never really felt like a kid because of the situation at home. He'd never known care-free. He'd hardly known fun until they'd both been free of his father's vitriol, his drunken stupors, and his abuse. If only—

Beth said, "You're quiet."

He could feel her eyes on him. In some ways that was exciting. In others, it just disconcerted him. "Just thinking. You do that too, don't you?"

She laughed and whatever tension had been there between them suddenly disappeared.

The restaurant they entered, *The Corner Cafe*, didn't look like much. In fact, on the outside it possibly looked like a joint. Being from the area, Sam knew differently.

This place had the best ribs in town.

The parking lot was at least half full, even for a mid-March day. Sam found himself guiding Beth inside by placing his hand in the small of her back. He found himself wanting to do more than that, but he remembered who she was, who he was, his career, and her history. That was a reality check he needed.

A table had just emptied toward the back. This was the type of place where you seated yourself. They headed for it of one accord. Wanting the privacy?

Maybe because the area would be a little quieter.

In no time at all, tall glasses of water with lemon were at their places, and menus were in their hands. Beth didn't hesitate to say, "Half a rack, baked potato, green beans, and applesauce."

Sam ordered a whole rack but the rest was the same.

"We should have brought bibs," she joked. "When I came here with Clare, they provided those little wet wipe towelettes, but they never quite do the job."

"You eat your ribs with a knife and fork?"

She rolled her eyes. "Puh-leeze. What real rib eater does?"

This time he laughed, and he found his eyes on hers. That shook him up a little.

She took a sip of her water and eyed him over the glass. "You asked me to lunch for a reason. What was it?"

"I can't just enjoy your company?"

She shrugged. "I suppose you can." However, she studied him in that way she had that encouraged him to confess the truth.

"I felt bad about the way I left on Wednesday."

"Why did you feel bad? It's not like we're dating or anything."

"Did your therapist teach you to ask so many questions?"

"Probably. And it's best always to clarify. Since I met Clare and my original family, I need straight answers. So I don't hesitate to ask."

He blew out a breath and fingered his knife. "What would you say if I told you I wanted to date you?" As she studied the glass-topped table, he wondered why her answer was so important to him. He almost seemed to be holding his breath.

"I told you I haven't dated anyone. I might not know how to go about it."

He relaxed a little. So that's what was troubling her. "It's been a long time since I dated anyone. We could figure it out together."

"Even if I'm consulting with a psychic?"

"I can keep an open mind."

"What does that mean?"

"It means that I don't know if I believe in psychics. On the other hand, I certainly don't have all the answers, and in my practice and in my travels, I've seen cause and effect that I can't explain."

"Gillian says it's all about energy."

"I was thinking about that," he confessed. "I pulled a shoulder muscle a couple of years ago. I have a friend who's an acupuncturist. He convinced me to let him try it. After about six treatments, the shoulder was better. He said that was because the energy had been blocked and he helped unblock it. Would it have healed on its own in that amount of time? Maybe. But I do know after each treatment I was more relaxed than I'd felt in years."

Suddenly Beth's phone played from in her jacket pocket. She looked apologetic. "It could be a client. I really should check and see who it is."

"No problem," he said, realizing most of her life was on the computer and phone.

She checked the screen and then mouthed to Sam, "It's Shara, Clare's daughter."

He nodded.

She listened and then she said, "Don't panic, Shara. Call your GYN. I'll be there as soon as I can."

She ended the call and looked at Sam. "Shara's spotting. Joe and Clare are away this weekend and she doesn't want to call them. Can you drop me at my place for my car?"

"No," he said without blinking an eye. "We'll go get her. A baby's involved. We shouldn't waste any time."

The look Beth gave him showed surprise, but something else too. He'd figure out what that was when this crisis was over.

Chapter Seven

Beth stood aside as Sam helped Shara into the back seat of his SUV. He lifted her legs and swung them in when she seemed to be having trouble.

"Are you having cramping?" he asked.

"A little," she said in a breathy voice. They both knew she was more scared than anything else.

"I'll ride in the back with her," Beth said, running around the vehicle and climbing in. Shara was six months pregnant and spotting could lead to her losing the baby. She'd found out recently she was having a girl.

As Beth slid next to Shara and held her hand, she heard Sam say," I'll get you there in no time. I promise."

There was that word again, Beth thought. Just what did promises mean to Dr. Sam Benedict? Some people said the word without much thought, but she had the feeling he knew exactly what he was saying.

By Shara's side, she asked, "Are you sure you don't want to call your mom? She really should know what's going on."

"I have my insurance info," Shara explained. "I don't need her here right this minute. If nothing's wrong, I don't want to panic her and Joe."

If nothing was wrong, they wouldn't be rushing Shara to the hospital.

Even though it was only mere minutes later, Beth felt as if she'd taken a long drive as Sam pulled up in front of the emergency department doors. With Amanda and Max gone, with Clare and Joe away, Beth felt the weight of a family connection to Shara. She felt responsible for her. It was an odd feeling she hadn't experienced since she and Hannah had been friends as teenagers.

"Stay put," Sam told Shara. "I'll get you a wheelchair."

When Shara didn't protest, Beth was really worried. The teenager looked pale and seemed a little clammy. Was it possible she'd lose the baby? Beth knew she had to stay calm, stay focused, stay sensible.

In no time at all Sam was there with the wheelchair. Beth assured him, "I'll wheel her in and get her registered if you want to park."

He nodded and went to do just that. But before he did, their gazes connected and again she realized what a caring man he was. Not just anyone would drop everything to take care of a practical stranger. Shara might be the granddaughter of a friend, but still—

Three hours later, Beth breathed a sigh of relief as she and Sam took Shara home and saw to her comfort on the sofa at Clare's house. Beth noticed that when Sam looked down at Shara, he did it as a father might. "Rest for a week means rest for a week. You either stay on the sofa or in bed. The doctor was clear about that."

"I won't move except to go to the bathroom," Shara vowed. "I'm so grateful everything's okay. It wasn't until I thought I might lose the baby that I realized how much I really want her. Dr. Knoll said in a week she'd do another ultra-sound. And if I don't have any spotting, I can resume normal activities again. I'm going to be scared until the baby is born."

"Being scared won't help the baby," Beth admonished. "How about instead of being scared, you research names you like. We can also figure out what you need for the layette. When you can resume normal activities again, I can take you shopping. I'm sure your mom and grand-mother would like to too."

"I can pick a theme for the baby's room," Shara de-cided. "I can look up decorations and bedding on-line."

"Right now you have to call your mother and tell her what's going on. I can stay here with you until they get home."

"All right," Shara agreed, taking out her phone. "But they're going to freak. You know they will."

"Your mom loves you and so does Joe."

With a sigh, Shara tapped her contact button and pressed the phone icon to dial her mom.

While she was doing that, Beth and Sam migrated into the kitchen. "I'm sure Clare left a full pantry when she and Joe left. I'll make us lunch." She checked her watch. "More like an early supper. I can't believe you changed your appointments so you could stay with us."

"I thought you might need help getting Shara home," Sam said with a shrug.

"You were a rock back at the hospital. Thank you."

"You were pretty sturdy yourself. You seemed to have a calm that sets in during a crisis."

"All that therapy again," she joked.

But Sam wouldn't let her get away with that. He gently held her arm and turned her to face him. "Therapy only works when the client is willing to learn and change. I don't think you give yourself enough credit."

They were standing very close, out of earshot, and out of sight of Shara. As Beth gazed up at Sam, she was aware of the trace scent of his citrusy aftershave, the wave of his hair over his brow, the crinkle lines around his eyes—those very blue eyes.

His voice was husky when he said, "I've never met anyone like you before."

How was that possible? He'd been all over the world. She wanted to say she was nothing special. She even wanted to say she was damaged. Couldn't he see that? Couldn't he see that she wasn't sure if she knew how to care for a man? That she didn't know if she could be intimate with a man?

As if Sam realized some of what was going through her head, he murmured, "Stop thinking and just feel."

Oh, she *felt* all right. She felt an attraction that scared her. She felt a need deep inside that awed her.

When he lowered his head, she was mesmerized and didn't move away. She did tense a little, however, not knowing how she'd react to the feel of his lips on hers. But he didn't kiss her lips. He kissed her cheek and then his mouth slid along the crease of her lips. She realized he was holding her lightly so she could escape easily if she wanted to. She didn't want to escape.

She hardly breathed, wondering what would come next. As Sam rubbed his cheek against hers, she felt the slightest bit of beard stubble. Finally, he rested his mouth against hers, pressed lightly, and they were kissing. Her arms went around his neck, and she held on, welcoming the pressure of his lips on hers, liking the feeling of being this close, straining up to him for more of what he had to offer. If that kiss had gone on forever, she wouldn't have objected. But it didn't. He slid his hands under her hair and along her neck, then pulled away.

Looking down at her, he asked gruffly, "How's that?"

Looking up at him, she felt speechless. Yet she knew she had to find some words before he thought she hadn't liked it. "That was an experience I've never had before, and I look forward to doing it again."

He laughed. "I don't know, Beth. Doing it again could lead us both into trouble. I don't do well with relationships. My lifestyle just isn't conducive to them."

"Then why did you kiss me?"

"Because you're honest clear through, because kissing you seemed the best idea in the world at that moment, because I like you, and seeing you again just seems to bring light into my world."

She smiled. "So are you going to stay for an early supper?"

"I will if you let me help make it."

"It's a deal."

And it seemed like the best deal she'd made in a very long time.

Clare's head was reeling as she watched Beth and the doctor leave and Joe go to his car for their suitcases. Their overnight get-away had turned into such a disaster. It had started out well enough. After they'd arrived at the hotel, they'd taken a bath together in the whirlpool tub. That had led them to the bed, and as always, Joe's love-making had taken her away from the ordinary and the mundane. She'd had trepidations about leaving Shara alone this weekend, but Joe had convinced her it would be okay.

Leaving *hadn't* been okay.

The only thing about coming home and seeing Shara ensconced on the sofa under a throw with her legs up, her expression worried, had been the vibes between Beth and Sam. Her sister hadn't been close to any man, except maybe her adoptive father. Beth had told her he'd always been supportive, made sure he was at an assembly when she won an award, encouraged her to be whatever she wanted to be. But Clare had still sensed some distance there. Clare's own dad and Beth were trying to establish a relationship, and every once in a while, Clare caught a glimpse in Beth's eyes of the child she'd once been, and the trust she'd had in their dad. But it was fleeting.

Maybe this Dr. Benedict could make all the difference in the world.

Now, as Clare turned toward the sofa and her daughter, she focused on what should be the most important at anytime...all the time. Shara's well-being.

She sat on the sofa next to Shara's legs and stared

straight into her daughter's eyes. "I'm sorry I left you alone this weekend."

"Mom, this wasn't your fault. It would have happened whether you were here or not."

"But I should have been here. I should have been the one to take you to the hospital. I don't want you for a minute to think you're alone in this pregnancy."

Shara looked down at her hands rather than at Clare. "I know I said I wanted to have this baby, Mom. I know I said I wanted to be a mother. But am I going to be able to do it?"

"With my help and your grandmother's, you will."

"I'm afraid you'll be the mom and I'll just be a big sister. When I thought I might lose her, I realized how much I want her. How am I going to make a life for her? How are we going to do this?"

Clare took her daughter's hand. "I know we have to plan some things, but there are others we can't plan. We'll have to take it day by day and see what happens. I'm sure there are going to be nights when you don't get any sleep, and you're going to wish you'd never become a mother. There are going to be days when you want a life other than that of a mom, but don't know how you can have it."

"You went through it," Shara murmured.

"I did, and my problem was I wouldn't accept help. Don't make that same mistake."

"But too much help won't be good for me or the baby. I won't know if I can stand on my own."

"You have to be strong enough and have the tools to stand on your own. If I come home from work and you need me to take care of my granddaughter so you can study, so be it. If you want to go to business school or college, and your grandmother decides to sell her business so she can babysit for you, say thank you and appreciate what she's giving you. Each time we make a decision, the three of us, we have to take everyone's needs into consideration and their capabilities. We have to be realistic about all of it. Just think about your little girl being raised by three women who love her to bits every day and want only the best for her."

"But what if we don't agree?" Shara asked mournfully. "You and Gram didn't get along for years. You and I weren't doing so great either before I ran away."

"This is now, not then," Clare assured her. "Your grandmother and I have come to an understanding, and Beth coming home has helped that."

"Because they forgot about you when they were trying to find Beth all those years."

"They didn't forget about me, but they were sad. After a while, they got lost in grieving for a daughter when they didn't know if she was dead or alive. I can understand better now what they felt, and they can understand what I felt."

"You don't expect Gramps to help raise my daughter?"

"I'm not sure yet what part he'll play. He was working all the time when I was little. As a child advocate lawyer, he helped kids even if he couldn't find his daughter. He works a lot now too. Child advocacy is important to him. So I'm not sure how much he'll be around, day to day."

"What about Joe?" Shara asked.

Clare wasn't sure how to answer that, and she didn't have to because right then Joe came in the door carrying her suitcase.

"I'll take it back to your room," he said. But then he added, "Why don't you come with me and we can talk for a few minutes."

Shara lifted the electronic tablet she had tucked beside her on the sofa. "Talk all you want. Don't worry about me. I'm searching for baby names."

Clare followed Joe to the bedroom where he hefted her suitcase onto the bed. "I know you're upset, but Shara's okay."

"We don't know that yet," Clare said, feeling emotion rise up in her. "After a week of bed rest, whatever this is might not resolve. She may still lose the baby. We shouldn't have gone anywhere."

When he came over to Clare, he tried to put his arms around her. But she backed away, not wanting his comfort right now. She was agitated and scared and confused.

He looked hurt. "We have to make some decisions, Clare. If you won't marry me now, then maybe we should move in together."

She wrapped her arms around herself tightly. "I can't believe you want me to make major life decisions when this is going on. Can't you see that Shara has to be my focus? Can't you see that I can't think about the rest when I don't know what's going to happen with her?"

Joe stepped over to the door and closed it. She knew why. Her voice had risen with each word, with each feeling, with each doubt.

"If anything, she needs stability, and we could give her that. You're running scared. You have been ever since we met and felt this attraction between us. I didn't move on it because I knew you weren't ready. But then when Shara ran away, we became closer, and I thought you *were* ready."

"We've only been dating four months."

"Dating?" Joe asked. "Is that what you call it? I thought we were building a relationship and a life. I almost lost mine several times in Afghanistan. I know the next minute could be my last. I don't want to wait for a life with you when I don't have to."

Clare was shaking her head. "We shouldn't talk about this now. I'm upset. You don't understand what I'm feeling."

"I *do* understand," he protested.

"How could you when you don't have children?"

He took a step back. "You think I need to have children to know how you feel?"

Tears burned in her eyes. "I'm not sure you can understand. Shara is my heart...my life."

"And at some point you're going to have to let her go on her own."

"Yes, at some point. But that point isn't now. She's going to need me and Mom and even Beth. She's too young to understand the responsibilities involved. She doesn't have the foresight or the experience to know what she's getting into."

"But you know and understand everything." He had an edge to his voice, and she could tell he was angry.

"I don't understand *everything*. But I certainly do understand what it's like to have a child without the father helping. I understand staying up at night, feeding, playing, buying groceries, getting from here to there with a car carrier and a diaper bag. When I did it, I was stubborn and rebellious and couldn't accept help. I want to make sure Shara has help."

"And you don't think I want that too? We've talked about this, Clare. If I take on you, I take on the Thaddeus family and its whole history."

"Take it on? Like a burden?" She latched onto that and she knew she probably shouldn't. But it had just hit her the wrong way.

"Are you purposely misunderstanding me?"

"Are you sure you know what you're getting into? You say you want to live together. Would we live here or in your house? Do you realize what it's like when a baby has colic and might be crying every day and night?"

"I understand sleep deprivation. PTSD will do that."

Joe did understand so much about life, about her, and maybe she was running scared. Yet she also knew she couldn't plan a life with him when hers was in such an upheaval.

"You said we could take this slow," she reminded him.

"Clare, I love you. Slow is one thing. Stalled is another."

She didn't respond. She couldn't. Falling in love with Joe had been wonderful. But now they were in the reality of the situation. She didn't know if he was ready for that reality. She didn't know if *she* was. Juggling a relationship or a marriage with him while raising her granddaughter? Could she do it?

She didn't respond, and Joe looked defeated when he said, "Maybe we need some space."

Her voice was tremulous when she agreed, "Maybe we do."

He didn't give her time to change her mind. He opened the bedroom door and walked out.

Chapter Eight

"Joe left, and you haven't talked to him since?" Beth had stopped in at her sister's on Monday afternoon to see Shara. She imagined bed rest wasn't any fun. But Shara was taking a nap after lunch and Clare had brewed coffee for her and Beth. That meant she wanted to talk. Beth had learned that about her sister early on.

"It's only been two days," Clare returned defensively.

"Do you usually go two days without speaking to Joe?"

Clare let out a sigh before she admitted, "No." She took a few sips of coffee and murmured, "He just doesn't understand."

"Maybe *you're* the one who doesn't understand. I know you feel as if you have a monumental responsibility to Shara now and tough decisions to make."

Clare began to speak, but Beth held up her hand. "However... Did you ever consider that Joe still feels like an outsider?"

That question stopped Clare. She protested, "He's *not* an outsider."

"You say that. But it's how Joe feels that matters," Beth went on. "Even though the Crandalls adopted me, I always had this outsider feeling. They never treated me like one. They always considered me their daughter. But deep down I knew they weren't my birth parents. When I was about twelve, I remember asking Mom if I could see the adoption decree. I studied that official document. Everyone had signed on the dotted line, so to speak. Their name was mine. That day I decided I *wasn't* an outsider. Maybe Joe needs an official document and the sanctity of marriage to feel as if he's really part of your life."

"But what if he comes inside my life and wants out again? What if it's too much to handle?"

"You don't trust him."

Clare was silent.

"Because Max left Amanda?"

"Yes, that," Clare breathed. "And Shara's father didn't want her. The father of her baby isn't interested in fathering, either. If Joe bails, Shara will feel that too."

"Don't you think Joe understands all that? If you keep pushing him away, he'll leave. Is that what you want?"

While Clare thought about that, Beth's cell phone played from her purse. Absentmindedly, Clare waved her hand at it. "Go ahead and take it."

When Beth checked her screen, she saw her dad was calling. She answered, "Hi, Dad, what's up?"

"Where are you?" Roger Crandall asked.

"I'm at Clare's."

"I'm at your apartment. Can you come home?"

"What are you doing here in York?"

"I have something for you. Your mother and I talked about it and we think we should give it to you," her dad said. "I told her I'd drive to York and back this time."

Beth felt torn between supporting Clare and seeing her dad. She said, "Wait a minute, Dad," and covered the phone. Then she told Clare, "My Dad says he brought me something he and my mother thought I should have. He's waiting at my apartment."

Clare didn't hesitate. "Tell him you're on your way. I'm fine, Beth, really. Just confused. I'll work it out. If your dad drove all this way from Pittsburgh, it must be important."

Beth's throat suddenly tightened at the understanding she heard in Clare's words. She responded in a thick voice, "I'm glad you're my sister."

Twenty minutes later, Beth pulled into the small back parking lot at *Yesteryear's Treasures*. When she ran around the building and up the side deck, she spotted her father sitting on a lawn chair outside her door. He stood as she came up the steps.

When she reached him, he gave her a hug. She found tears come into her eyes, but that was silly.

He leaned away and asked, "How are you?"

She answered honestly, "Still taking it all in."

He nodded to her face where her scar had been. "It's all gone."

"I'm working on it," she concluded and she could see he understood.

Her car's remote still in her hand, she found the apartment door key on the ring and opened the door.

A breeze chilled her through her jacket. Or maybe the chill originated with the anticipation of learning whatever her dad had come to give her.

"Coffee?" she asked, as he shrugged out of his jacket.

"How about hot chocolate?" he suggested, with a twinkle in his eye. Whenever her parents had something serious to discuss, they did it over hot chocolate.

Her dad, unlike Max, wasn't used to wearing suits and ties. He'd been a blue collar worker all his life. A plumber by trade, he ran his own firm, but he still went out on jobs with his men, doing everything from replacing faucets to planning a water system for a new house.

Roger Crandall was about five years older than Max. His hair was medium brown with strands of grey shining silver in the bright daylight. Each year he lost a little more hair on the top of his head. He was husky at five foot ten, and preferred flannel shirts until he discarded them for summer cotton plaids. He'd always been a solid supporting force in Beth's life even when she'd still been afraid of him. His caring and kindness had coaxed her into trusting him.

"Hot chocolate it is," she assured him with an answering smile.

He glanced around the apartment. "Your mother said you've really settled in."

"For now. I like the apartment. But if Amanda sells *Yesteryear's Treasures*, I'll have to find another place. If I stay in York," she added.

Quickly she found a pot, poured in two cups of milk and set it on a burner to warm. Then she pulled the tin of cocoa and a bottle of vanilla from the cupboard.

"Your mom mentioned that. It's quite a sacrifice for Amanda to think of caring for Shara's baby full time so Clare can still work and Shara can go to school."

"I don't believe Amanda sees it as a sacrifice. She seems excited about being a great grandmom."

"Maybe she can find someone to run the business for her. That could be as easy as selling it. The Thaddeus family will figure it out." He stopped after he said that and added softly, "You're one of them now."

"I'm still a Crandall," she insisted.

"But you were a Thaddeus first, and your mother tells me digging up the past could bring your old memories into light again. I'm worried for you, honey."

While they'd talked, Beth had stirred the cocoa in the saucepan, adding vanilla and sugar to the milk. Now she poured it into two mugs and brought it to the small table. Sitting across from her dad, she patted his hand. "I have to do this. I have to try to find Hannah. It's important."

"That's why I'm here."

Her dad had hung his jacket on the back of the chair. Now he reached into the pocket and laid a large red button on the table in front of Beth.

She knew her eyes held lots of questions when she looked up at him. It looked familiar. "What is it?"

"Do you remember the night you visited Hannah at the group home and then you were taken to the hospital because of the knife wound?"

She unsteadily said, "I remember Chuck and his knife. I remember him hurting me and Hannah saving me. I remember holding onto Hannah because I didn't want to leave without her."

"When your mother found you in the emergency department cubicle, you had this button clutched in your hand. You told her it was from Hannah's coat. She took it from you while they stitched you up."

"And she kept it all this time?"

"She pocketed it and forgot about it. After you came home, she didn't want to bring it up or any bad memories by asking you about it. By then we knew Hannah had been transferred somewhere else."

"To protect her," Beth murmured.

"Or to keep her from getting into trouble again with that crowd. We know you're looking for the proverbial needle in the haystack, but your mother told me about Gillian Bradley and your belief in her. We know this button was from Hannah's coat. If it could help— Well, here it is."

Taking the button in her hand, Beth closed it into her palm. "Thank you."

"No thanks necessary, honey. We just want to see you happy. That's all we've ever wanted." He reached out and squeezed her other hand. "I've missed you," he said soberly. "But I know you need to find out who you really are and who you want to be."

She closed her eyes for a moment, thinking about all of it—thinking she should call Gillian. But when she opened her eyes again, she saw the man she'd called Dad since she was three watching her with concern.

"Why don't you stay tonight?" she asked him.

He shook his head. "I can't. Your mom will worry."

"Not if you call."

"I'll tell you what. I'll stay for dinner. We'll order pizza with all that goop you like on it. That will give us a few hours to talk about everything ... and nothing. Then I'll drive home. I can be there by midnight."

"That sounds good," she agreed, knowing her adoptive parents didn't like to be away from each other for long. That's the kind of marriage she wanted some day.

Marriage. Was that the first time she'd considered it? Maybe so.

Her father texted her mother his plans and she texted back. She told him that he should enjoy his visit, take his time driving, and be careful. He and Beth took their hot chocolate into the living room and began to catch up. She had decided to let her call to Gillian wait until tomorrow. One more day wouldn't make a difference.

Their time sped by as though their words had wings— from his plumbing jobs to her mother wanting to plant a garden this summer to Clare's situation with Shara.

Finally her dad asked, "Do you still have nightmares?"

She'd had them consistently until about seven years into her therapy when they'd eased up and then, for the most part stopped. Her therapist had suggested she'd finally felt safe.

Feeling safe had been everything to her, perhaps even more important than feeling loved. Yet they'd possibly gone hand in hand.

"I had a nightmare the first night I slept here. But none since. For some reason I feel safe in this apartment now. And it's not just because of the alarm system.

Maybe Amanda's good vibes are here."

"Do you ever think you'll call her Mom again?"

"It's possible."

Knowing that was dangerous territory to speculate about, she rose from the sofa and went to the refrigerator door in the kitchen for the pizza menu. She handed it to him. "Want to split a baked ziti and meatballs with that pizza?"

"Only if you don't tell your mom."

"Deal," she agreed with a grin.

However, before she could pick up the phone to call in their order, her phone burbled. It did that when a text came in. She quickly read it since it was from Sam. It was short and to the point. **Go with me to the fund-raising gala Friday night? Formal.**

A formal gala with Sam? She had nothing suitable to wear. She never dressed up like that. But Clare or Shara would know what to do if she needed advice.

Her better judgment told her to pass and tell Sam "no," but her heart...her heart urged her to text him back and she did. **Yes, I'll go. E-mail details.**

"Who was that?" her dad asked as she set down her phone.

"It was Sam Benedict. He's the doctor—"

"Who fixed your face," her dad cut in. "Your mother told me about him. Now I want *you* to tell me about him. Will you?"

Thinking about the idea, she decided who better to discuss Sam with than her dad?

"Let me order that pizza then I'll tell you everything I know and you can give me your opinion."

"About?"

"About whether or not I should date him."

Because that's where she and Sam were headed, and they both knew it.

Beth phoned Gillian after her father left instead of in the morning. After all, Gillian was on the West Coast and it wouldn't be as late there. Her hands were shaking as she did it. The button sat on the end table next to her sofa, calling her eyes to it over and over again. She fully intended to leave a voice message.

But Gillian answered. "Hi, Beth, how are you?"

"I'm good. I want to find Hannah, no matter what memories come up."

"I see. So you want to meet with me?"

"I do. And I have something that might help us. All these years my mom kept a button that I pulled off Hannah's coat. Can that help us find her?"

"It might. Do you think your therapist will meet with us too?"

Beth had also thought about that idea. "I'd rather do this without her."

"Beth…"

"Really, Gillian, I'd like Amanda and Clare to be there."

"What if you have your therapist on call?"

Beth knew Gillian was concerned about her emotional well being. "I can do that. Amanda and Max return on Wednesday. When can *you* get free?"

"I'll check with Nathan to see what his schedule looks like. We don't have Dana and Maddie again until the end of April. Maybe I can fly in over the weekend and we can go from there."

"That sounds good."

"This button that you have. Don't let anyone else handle it, and put it someplace…soft."

"Soft?"

"I know that sounds funny, but I don't want it clanging around with other objects."

"My mother had it in her jewelry box."

"A jewelry box is fine, or wrap it in a handkerchief if you slip it into a drawer."

Beth studied the button. "I can do that."

"And, Beth. I want you to be hopeful but realistic too."

"I understand."

"I'll give you a call back as soon as I check with Nathan, then you can see what will suit your therapist."

"Thank you."

"I haven't done anything yet," Gillian reminded her.

"But you're going to try. That's what matters."

"I'll talk to you soon," Gillian said softly as she ended the call.

The button became Beth's focus again. What she remembered most was wanting to be like Hannah— tough, courageous, a fighter.

Beth had become a fighter in her own way. Just what would Hannah be like now?

After Clare got home from work the following day, she picked up Beth and drove her to a specialty boutique in York—*Evening in Paris*.

"We shouldn't have come," Beth protested. "You could be with Shara."

"We're ten minutes away and Becky's with her. Becky is the one friend who stood by her through everything and they need time together too." She glanced around the interior of the dress shop. "You have a great figure, though you hide it. This won't take long."

"I should have told Sam *no*. I don't know why I agreed to go. I don't like crowds—"

"But you like Sam Benedict. I wished he'd realized you need more than a few days to prepare. Are you going to let me do your hair on Friday?"

When Beth hesitated, Clare added to the pot. "Shara and I can help with your make-up too. You can get dressed at our place."

After Beth thought about the idea, she agreed. "Maybe doing my makeup will take Shara's mind off everything else."

Going deeper into the shop, Beth stopped, disconcerted by the rack of formal wear—the gowns with sequins. "I just want a little black dress!"

Clare was already shaking her head. "Nonsense. Black is old. I think you should go for red, and really wow Dr. Benedict."

Beth held out her hand like a stop sign. "I don't want to *wow* him. I just don't want to embarrass myself."

With a long studying look, Clare decided, "You don't want to turn him on."

"Clare—" Beth's voice held a warning.

A woman dressed in a purple sheath and five-inch spiked heels came up to them.

Just how did she walk in those shoes without toppling over or cramping her toes? Beth wondered.

The clerk asked, "How can I help you today?"

Clare pointed to Beth. "This is my sister. We're going to dress her up for a formal event, something long with sequins and high strappy heels."

"No," Beth protested so loudly the salesclerk jumped.

But the woman recovered quickly. "What color do you have in mind?"

"Don't say black," Clare warned.

With a sigh, Beth decided, "Blue. I like most shades of blue."

Clare wrinkled her nose. "Only if it has an exciting design or something see-through. If not that, then fuchsia."

"No see-through," Beth said firmly.

After the clerk looked from one to the other, she invited them, "Come with me. I'm sure we can find something you like."

Beth tried on seven dresses, from short to long, with a slit and without, one with sequins and another with glass beads. She finally decided on a teal, one-shouldered short dress with beading along the shoulder and neckline. Clare thought the dress was sedate. But to Beth, it was daring. She'd never worn anything like it before or wanted to.

To her surprise, she gave into Clare's suggestion of modestly high-heeled silver shoes that showcased crisscross straps over her foot and around her ankle. Unlike Cinderella, she couldn't step out of one. The clerk insisted they were very in-trend. A beaded silver purse and a sparkly shawl completed the outfit.

As they left the shop, Clare checked her watch. "An hour and fifteen minutes. And I called Shara while you were in the middle of trying everything on. She's fine. She and Becky have been catching up. I told her we'd pick up Chinese. Okay with you?"

Beth realized again that she liked having a sister. The feeling when Clare shepherded her into something reminded her of a long time ago when she and Clare had built sand castles on the beach and Clare had whispered secrets in her ear. It also reminded her of a friendship with Hannah. She remembered whenever Hannah had slept over at her house, they'd huddled together and talked about music and dreams.

"I like Chinese," she answered her sister, grateful they'd found each other again.

Now she just had to find Hannah.

Chapter Nine

On Friday, Beth allowed Clare and Shara to supervise her hairstyling and makeup application. But then she drove to her apartment to dress and wait for Sam. When he appeared at her door, she was suddenly stricken with what an actor might term stage-fright.

"What's wrong?" he asked. "You're as pale as a ghost."

"I think I made a mistake."

He looked totally perplexed. "What kind of mistake?"

"I don't think I should have agreed to go with you tonight."

At her words, his expression relaxed a little, but just a little. He took her hand and led her into the living room. He motioned to the sofa. "Sit, and tell me what this is about."

"You look so dashing." Those were the only words she could think of though it sounded very dramatic.

He gave a chuckle. "And that's a bad thing?"

He'd looked great in a suit at Amanda and Max's wedding, but tonight, he was wearing a tuxedo-type suit without a cummerbund but with a bow tie. His crisp white shirt practically dazzled her, but not as much as his blue eyes. She blurted out, "You're going to be perfectly comfortable there. You know these people. You fit in. I don't."

Easing close to her on the sofa, he took her hand in his. "Did you look in the mirror after you got dressed?"

"Just a glimpse," she admitted. "Shara and Clare fixed my hair and helped me do my makeup. I came home and slid into my dress. So, no, I didn't take much of a look."

He shook his head. "You are so unlike any other woman I know."

"See what I mean? I'm not going to belong."

"That is a *compliment*, Beth. You look absolutely fantastic. That dress makes my mouth water." His face reddened a bit. "Uh oh. I shouldn't have said that. It will make you panic even more."

His complete honesty disarmed her, and she took a long breath. "I really look okay? Shara and Clare said I did, but I knew they wanted me to feel good about everything. I don't usually—" She motioned to her hair and makeup, dress and shoes. "Do all this."

"Then why did you do it?"

"Because...because they said I should. They said I should wow you."

Now he laughed out loud. "You have seriously wowed me. Why don't you think you'll fit in? Just because you haven't done it before?"

"Crowds make me panic a little, especially crowds where I don't know anybody."

"But you will know somebody. You'll know *me*."

He had her there. "What if I have a panic attack in the middle of all those people and embarrass you?"

"Do you have panic attacks often?"

"No, not for years. But that's basically because I work from my apartment and don't see anybody but family."

"Have you ever thought about changing that aspect of your life?" Now the humor was gone from his tone and it was a significant question.

"I've thought about it, but never quite knew how to go about it. Or had the motivation."

"Do you think enough of me to have the motivation tonight?"

Wow. Wasn't that cutting to the core of it? "So what you're saying is, if I stop thinking about me and I start thinking about you, everything will be fine."

A slow smile stole across his lips. "Exactly. Think about the cause. Think about the charity. This is an event to raise money for kids who'd never be able to have surgery otherwise. I'll be talking to some people I'm hoping will be big-hearted in their donations. Believe it or not, conversation does help. Getting to know the doctors personally helps. Getting to know the woman behind the new website could help. There could be business owners who want your input, or fellow web designers you can chat with. You'll get a broader outlook on everything."

"But I never will if I stay in my apartment and only talk to family."

"Exactly."

She gnawed on her lower lip and wondered if she'd have to redo her lipstick. Enough time for that after she had something to eat because then it would need to be redone anyway.

"All right, let's go. If I get nervous, I'll just think about the kids."

"You're a courageous woman, Beth Crandall."

"I don't know how you can say that. I almost just bailed on you."

"But the point is, you didn't. I have a feeling you never have."

Since she didn't know what to say to a compliment like that, she murmured, "I'll get my shawl."

A minute later she came out of her bedroom and saw that the living room was empty. Sam had migrated to the kitchen and she joined him there.

When she unfolded the shawl to wrap it around her shoulders, he took it from her. The sparkly thread running through the shawl complemented the bling on her dress. Facing her, he wrapped it around her shoulders, touching her ever so slightly in the process. A tremble danced up her arms and she realized that tremble wasn't from fear. It was from anticipation. She actually *liked* Sam touching her.

That was as much a surprise as going to this gala tonight. Maybe she stayed in her apartment and never tried to date because she'd always been afraid of what would happen if she did—afraid of her own reactions, afraid memories would come rushing back, afraid she'd never be normal. No, she didn't remember what had happened to her. She didn't know if the man who had kidnapped her had abused her sexually. That was part of the problem. If she didn't know, how could she heal? Her adoptive parents had helped her overcome this scared feeling, though it had taken years. Panic had become a thing of the past except in some new situations. But she knew from being secreted from her home in the middle of the night by a stranger, held captive, dumped in a busy mall where she'd become even more scared by all the people milling about her... She'd always known she was different. She'd always felt something was wrong with her. She'd realized that sometimes she had to work twice as hard to do what normal people did with ease.

Sam was studying her. "Do you believe me when I tell you you look beautiful and you'll be able to hold your own against any other woman who's there tonight?"

"That's going a little far. How about, I look presentable, and I'll do my best to think about anybody but me, and make them feel comfortable. That way I can aid your cause and not hurt it. That way I have a purpose."

"And a purpose helps?"

"More than you know."

He brought her in close and just held her for a few seconds. He didn't try to kiss her. He didn't try to give her anything but comfort. He murmured into her hair, "You do get a good meal out of tonight—cocktails, appetizers, and even dessert."

She leaned away from him and smiled, a genuine smile. "Well, that settles it. Let's go."

Sam drove to York...into the downtown area. The gala was being held at the Yorktowne Hotel. They parked in the parking garage and then Sam walked her across the street and inside the historic building. The Yorktown Hotel, according to Clare, was a historic treasure. It had been built in 1925 and had its roots in the history of the Roaring Twenties. The architecture was renaissance-revival style. At eleven stories, it featured twenty-foot high ceilings, ornate brass and crystal chandeliers, and wood-paneled rooms. The huge wall-sized mirrors added to the luxurious ambience.

As she and Sam roamed through the reception area, Beth couldn't get enough of the elegantly appointed décor. She understood she must look like a little kid in a candy shop.

Sam had taken her hand and tucked it into his elbow. He said, "Did you know York was once called Yorktowne?"

"I think I read that before I came here for the first time."

"And you know it functioned as the nation's capital when Philadelphia was under British occupation."

"Amanda seemed very proud of that fact."

"Probably because the Continental Congress adopted the Articles of Confederation here in York."

"I'm used to history. We have it in Pittsburgh too," she said dryly.

Sam squeezed her hand. "Just giving you a little background."

"So you were born and raised here?"

"I was," Sam said, but didn't elaborate. And Beth had the feeling he might not unless she strongly prompted him the same way he prompted her.

Sam seemed to know everyone—donors, colleagues, even hotel staff. As they sat at a round table, eating Sam's dinner selection for them—almond encrusted flounder—she asked, "I guess you've had fundraisers here before?"

"At least once a year. And when I can, I attend professional functions here."

"You really do have your foot in two worlds, don't you? One foot on foreign soil when you're helping children in another country, and the other when you're back here doing PR."

"I have a practice here too, remember?" he said in a light voice though she could sense a bit of an edge behind it.

She touched her face reflexively. "Yes, I know you do. And I imagine there are plenty of children in the United States who could use your help. Why the foreign countries?"

"Because they're the forgotten ones."

She studied him and he obviously became uncomfortable with her perusal. Seeing she was finished with her main course too, he said, "Let's dance."

"That's an avoidance technique," she warned him.

"There are too many people here and too much distraction to have a serious conversation."

"I'll remind you of that when we're alone."

He shook his head and smiled. "I can see I can't get away with anything with you, can I?"

"Not much," she assured him.

This time when they danced, unlike at Amanda and Max's wedding reception, they were more comfortable with each other. He took her into his arms easily and held her a little closer than he had at the wedding reception. He looked down at her as if asking if she were comfortable. She just gave him a little nod. She was fine. Very fine.

They didn't speak as they danced. They gazed into each other's eyes for a while and then Beth laid her cheek against the expensive fabric of Sam's jacket. His arm held her a little tighter.

"I'd like to kiss you again," Sam murmured at her ear. "But I don't want to embarrass you in front of all these people."

"I don't know them," she reminded him as she looked up at him. "On the other hand, I think I'd like to be someplace quiet with you when you do it again."

He rubbed his lips against her cheek where her scar had been. She wondered if that was intentional, or if it was just where his lips landed. She found the gesture tender and exciting, and knew she wanted to kiss Sam too, longer than before, maybe even deeper than before. What would happen if she did? Would she be okay? Or would some kind of awful memories come flooding back?

Maybe that was her biggest fear.

"You're thinking again," Sam whispered.

"You can tell?"

"You get very quiet, and I can sense you disappear away from me."

No one had ever put it exactly that way before. Sam actually seemed to get her in ways other people, including family in her life, couldn't.

Throughout the evening Beth found it fairly easy to speak with Sam's friends and colleagues about their work. She asked tons of questions. She'd learned to deflect attention away from herself that way and it usually paid off because people loved to be listened to, especially when they talked about something they were passionate about. Helping kids was the common bond here, and Beth could easily relate and be compassionate about that.

As they left the hotel at the end of the evening, Beth realized she'd had a good time. They'd navigated the parking garage and settled in Sam's SUV again when he asked, "So what did you think?"

"About the hotel, about your friends and colleagues, about your work?"

"Oh, I see I need to be more specific with you. About all of it," he joked.

"I'm glad you invited me if that's what you're really asking."

He was silent for a moment and then started up the engine. "Maybe that's what I was asking and I didn't know it."

As they pulled out of the parking garage, he said, "You told me you don't like crowds. I didn't want you to feel claustrophobic."

"I didn't. Maybe it was because of the high ceilings," she teased. "Or maybe because I was distracted by the beautiful surroundings."

"I think you got me a few more donors by talking about your own surgery and what it meant to you."

That had just happened in one of the conversations with a group of obviously affluent donors. She'd told them she could only imagine how grateful the children were when Sam and the other doctors helped. That's when she'd revealed Sam had done surgery for her and how it had taken away teenage trauma.

"I meant everything I said."

"So you feel making your scar fade helped your memories fade?"

"It's not about me forgetting what happened because the scar's gone now. The feelings associated with it are different. Before, I felt like what had happened, as well as the scar, marred me for life. Now I know it didn't. I have you to thank for that."

"Any plastic surgeon could have done it," he murmured.

She reached over and touched his arm. "But not just any plastic surgeon did."

After they reached Beth's apartment, Sam walked her upstairs. "I want to see you in," he said. "Unless you'd rather I didn't come in this late."

It was around midnight but the lateness and the darkness had nothing to do with whether she wanted Sam to come in or not. "Come on in," she said. "You can take off your jacket and loosen your tie, and we can have that conversation we couldn't have when we were dancing."

"I thought it was a kiss we didn't have," he said.

"Maybe we should see how the conversation goes."

He frowned. "You know, you can be a bit frustrating at times."

"And I suppose you're not? Coffee, tea, soda?"

"None of the above."

She nodded and followed him into the living room where he did as she suggested. He shrugged out of his jacket and laid it over the back of a chair. Then he untied the bowtie and let it hang around his collar.

"My father hates dressing up like that," Beth said.

"Max or your adoptive dad?"

"My adoptive dad. As you know, Max wears suits all the time."

"And your adoptive dad?"

"He likes casual shirts and a bottle of beer."

"I've been known to drink a beer or two."

She gave him a quick glance and he shrugged. "Just wanted to let you know I'm not a snob. What does your adoptive dad do?"

"He's a plumber. He has his own firm but he still goes out on jobs and works with his men."

"And your mom is a nurse?"

"Yes, she is, and one of the most caring people I know." Thinking about her parents and her dad's visit, she realized she hadn't yet told Sam about Hannah and the button." Now she said, "My mother had kept a button that I'd pulled from Hannah's coat the night I was taken to the hospital. Gillian thinks it could help locate Hannah, so she's going to fly in to meet with me tomorrow."

"Tomorrow? Are you ready for that?"

"As ready as I can be."

"And your mother kept that button all these years?"

"Yes. Apparently she'd slipped it into her pocket. I was clutching it when I came to the hospital. She forgot about it until afterward and then she didn't want to remind me about what had happened. So she just kept it in her jewelry box all these years."

"And you really think this is going to help Gillian?" There was doubt in his voice.

"You don't?"

"I'm a man of science, Beth. I believe in what I can see and do and study and touch. The idea that Gillian picks up energy from out of the air and then somehow reads it blows my mind."

Because of Gillian's history and the foundation she and her partner had set up, Beth had given this matter much thought. "Energy *is* scientific. Everyone is made of energy, communicates energy, sends energy. So why wouldn't someone gifted be able to pick it up and read it?"

Considering her words, Sam nodded. "Put that way, I suppose it's possible."

This doctor was good at tact. She pressed, "But you still don't believe it."

"I reserve judgment until you see what happens with Gillian. I don't want you to be disappointed."

"I've had many disappointments in my life, Sam. Most times I've just had to choose to hope rather than to be disappointed and regretful. So I'm hopeful about a meeting with Gillian."

Without a word, Sam slipped an arm around Beth's shoulders. He'd opened the collar and top button on his shirt. She could see curly black hairs springing there. An overwhelming desire to touch them overtook her. In addition, she longed for him to kiss her. Yet she'd invited him inside for more than a kiss and the quiet.

Before he could bend his head and start something that she didn't know the ending to, she asked, "Can you tell me something about how you grew up and your parents? You know everything about me. I don't know much about you."

With a furrow in his brow, Sam seemed to war with himself. She saw his eyes darken and his lips tighten. The nerve in his jaw worked and she had no idea what was going to come out of his mouth. Maybe he wouldn't answer her. He could just leave. But if he did, that meant they didn't have a chance—not at trust or at anything more.

Maybe he sensed that. Maybe he already did know her well enough to suspect that honesty was everything to her. Or maybe he thought shock value would keep her from asking more questions.

Dropping his arm from around her shoulders, he sat up straighter. "I had an abusive father, and a mother who wouldn't stand up for the two of us. My father punched first and asked questions later. My mother was too weak to act, too scared to realize that a child had to be protected. That's why I want to make sure children are heard and fixed when they can be."

There was a story in Sam's eyes that he didn't want to tell her. She could easily see that. How did he escape that vicious cycle? Had his mother escaped? Or had something awful happened to everyone?

Silence pervaded the room as she waited.

"Now you want the whole story," he grumbled.

"As much of it as you want to tell me. I'm not going to drag it out of you, Sam. That's not what sharing is about."

"You've had too much counseling. Too much for *my* good, anyway."

"You don't have to say another word," she assured him.

"But if I don't, another kiss between us isn't going to mean much, is it?"

"I can't answer that," she said softly.

He blew out a long breath. "I'm not proud of what finally happened. I'm still not at peace with any of it after all these years. Maybe I never will be. When things don't end well, how can you not have regrets?"

He didn't want her to answer that, not really. So she kept silent.

He ran his hand through his hair, mussing it. He obviously needed a moment to gather his thoughts. He began, "I finally got old enough and strong enough and angry enough to stand up for me and my mother. I was sixteen. My father came home one Friday night from his favorite bar loaded for bear. He'd given me black eyes and more bruises than I wanted to count. I'd taken it because I knew it would be worse for Mom if I didn't. He'd beaten her too, but the same was true there. If she asked for help or I did, I knew it would be worse for all of us...at least that's what my teenage mind thought until that Friday night."

When he stopped, Beth realized how difficult it was for him to go on. Yet she didn't feel the freedom yet to just reach over and touch him.

"I had a job at a burger joint," he continued. "When I came home, I heard arguing and yelling inside, then I heard Mom scream. I burst into the kitchen and saw her on the floor. My father was kicking her. I saw red like I've never seen red before or since. I went at him like a prize fighter. I don't know how much damage I did but I broke his nose. While he fell to his knees screaming like a baby, I called 9-1-1. They didn't put me in juvie because what I had done was considered self-defense. The police and I convinced Mom to press charges and file a restraining order. We went to a shelter for a while. When Mom was back on her feet again, we moved to Lancaster. The shelter had connections for jobs and she got a new one, working in a bakery."

He stopped and Beth had a feeling the rest of the story was going to get worse.

After a glance at her, Sam blew out a breath. "I don't talk about this. I don't tell anybody my history."

Suddenly there were no barriers between her and Sam. Somehow she had to show him she understood...and cared. She laid her hand on his thigh, a more intimate gesture than she was used to giving.

He studied her hand and he covered it with his. "I'd gotten another job, too, as a busboy in a restaurant. When I got home that night, there were police cars everywhere. My father had shot and killed my mother."

Beth gasped. She couldn't help it. "Oh, Sam."

He shook his head as if he didn't want sympathy. She knew he didn't want pity.

"My father died in a prison fight when I was in college," he said evenly.

"How did you handle all of it? You were so young."

"I had a teacher who'd taken an interest in me, maybe suspecting about my home life. He helped me get emancipated. After my mother was killed, I stayed in a room at his house for a while until I graduated from high school. He made sure I got scholarships. Thank God I'd always kept my grades up. In college I wasn't sure what I wanted to do, but I had a knack for science. Again with William's encouragement, I managed to get into med school. And the rest, as they say, is history."

She squeezed his hand. "Do you blame yourself?"

When his eyes locked to hers, he asked, "You really *do* understand, don't you? Of course, I blame myself. I started that whole end ball rolling."

"And if you hadn't? What would have happened the next Friday night or the next? Would he have killed your mom then instead of later? Maybe have killed you?"

"I tell myself that's possible. I tell myself that was even likely."

"But it doesn't help."

"It helps, some. We learn to live with questions and regrets, don't we?"

Studying him, she agreed. "We do, but not without consequences, even if they're good consequences."

"Good consequences?" He sounded puzzled.

"Yes. I suspect that in your work you're in large part trying to put good karma out there to make up for the bad karma you experienced."

"You think I'm trying to make up for what I did?"

"I didn't say that, Sam. I think you want to do good. I think you're trying to fix yourself from everything that happened."

"But?"

"But are you really happy?"

"I don't stop to think about happiness. The work I do gives me satisfaction and fulfillment."

"Is that enough?"

Turning to her again, wrapping his arm around her, he admitted, "I thought it was until I met you."

They hadn't known each other that long, yet it felt as if they had.

"Do you think less of me because I physically hurt someone else?" he asked and she understood how important her answer was to him. This must be a worry when he got involved with anyone. Did he feel unlovable because of what he thought was a sin?

"Let me put it this way," she said. "If Max could have beaten the heck out of the man who kidnapped me, he would have. If my adoptive father could have been in the same room with Luther Brown, he might have wrung his neck. You were protecting your mother and yourself with righteous anger. No, I don't think less of you."

"Nothing like that has ever happened again," Sam said in a low voice. "In the refugee camps, I've had to keep a gun nearby on occasion."

"Because of everything that's happened to me, I can get a good sense of someone when I'm with them. I trust my gut."

He gazed into her eyes, trying to read her deepest thoughts. "And what's your gut saying about me?"

She smiled. "It's saying something different than it's ever said before. It's saying that especially after tonight, I can trust you. It's telling me you're a kind, compassionate, strong man who knows how to share."

"Beth," he said in a voice that was sort of a growl but maybe a plea too.

She didn't wait for him to kiss her, she kissed him. The first time ever in her life she'd made that forward a move. But when she set her lips on his, he took over. She liked that about him. He was masterful, protective, and passionate...not only about his work.

She rode his passion along with hers. She let him taste

her and she tasted him until his hand went to her breast and rested there. He slowly rubbed his thumb over her. She leaned into him, excited by the sensations but scared too. Then he let his hand slide to her waist and he ended the kiss.

"Do you know what you're getting into?" he asked gruffly.

She blinked and thought about it. "No. I don't know if I can make love with a man...with you. On the other side of that, if we do, I guess we'd be having an affair."

When she saw him frown, she wasn't sure why. Maybe he didn't like the term? She wasn't sure *she* did.

"That's putting it in black and white terms," Sam said.

"We need to be able to see in black and white to know where we're going."

"We're not going to settle that tonight." He leaned forward, kissed her again, and then rose to his feet. "I'd better go while I can. I'll call you."

"Clare told me that men *say* that but don't *mean* it."

"I mean it."

She believed him.

Chapter Ten

When Sam called Beth Saturday morning, he asked, "Are you ready for your session with Gillian today?"

"I am. Gillian is flying in this afternoon. Amanda's having dinner at their house and I'll meet with Gillian there."

"Are you nervous?"

"Yes. Gillian made me promise to have my therapist on call, and I contacted Linda. But I'm hoping it's not necessary."

"Gillian seems thorough."

"She is." When there was silence, she wondered if Sam might like to join everyone for dinner. The worst he could do was say "no." She told herself she wouldn't be disappointed. "Would you like to come to dinner with me?"

There was a long pause. Finally, he said, "Dinner with Amanda and Max sounds good. I wouldn't mind being there when you meet with this Gillian. What time should I pick you up?"

"Around five?"

"Five is good."

That evening when she and Sam arrived at Amanda and Max's new house, she admired it. The sprawling one-story had a great room with a cathedral ceiling. The fireplace went from floor to ceiling and a dining area was located off the large kitchen. Three bedrooms nestled down a hall. After they joined Max, Amanda, Clare and Shara in the great room, Beth felt a little self-conscious. Why?

Because everyone was watching her and Sam.

He'd dressed casually this evening in khakis and a black Henley shirt. Since wearing her break-out dress to the gala, Beth had found herself gravitating more toward color than the navy and white she usually wore. She'd bought herself slim-legged jeans and a violet-colored tunic sweater for tonight.

"It's so nice of you to come," Amanda said to Sam, breaking the silence. "I hope you like roast beef and mashed potatoes."

"What red-blooded man doesn't?" Sam joked.

Max shook his hand. "It's been a long time."

"Before my last trip to Central America," Sam confirmed.

"You've met Shara, I hear, and Clare too."

Sam nodded to Clare and then asked Shara, "How are you feeling?"

"Much better. I'm off bed rest. Thanks for helping me out that day."

"No problem."

Glancing at Sam, Beth realized he really meant that. Sam helped because that was just who he was.

Amanda took Beth aside while the others were talking and asked, "Is this a date?"

Beth smiled. "Sort of."

"You know he's dedicated to his work."

"I do." Beth thought about their kisses and how she'd felt, the fact that she might want more than a few dates with Sam. How would his work play into all of that?

Apparently realizing she shouldn't say more, Amanda leaned in close again, changed the subject and whispered, "I think Clare needs some cheering up."

"Joe's not coming?"

"That's the problem. She didn't ask him. I don't know what's going on between those two, but they need to resolve it. Have you heard from Gillian?"

"I have. She texted when she landed. She should be here in about a half hour if traffic from BWI isn't too heavy."

"I'm going to check on dinner," Amanda said. "Maybe you can talk to Clare before Gillian arrives."

"About?"

"What she should do next."

"I certainly don't have any advice in the relationship department."

"No, but you could listen. It might help her sort out what she's thinking."

Beth knew that could be true. Seeing that Sam and Max were embroiled in a conversation, now might be a good time to talk to her sister.

As if Shara sensed the sisters needed to talk, she asked Amanda, "Need help in there?"

"You could put together a salad for us."

Once Shara had gone into the kitchen with Amanda, Beth said to Clare, "Let's go into the spare bedroom so we can talk."

Clare looked defiant for a moment. "About?"

"About whatever is putting that frown on your face."

"Talking won't do any good," she murmured, obviously in a down mood.

"You never know," Beth assured her hopefully. "Come on." She took her sister's hand.

Something about that gesture brought back memories of other times when they'd held hands. It was sort of a déjà vu feeling but nice. She knew, in a way, Clare had blamed herself for Beth's kidnapping. Not because she could have prevented it, but because she was the older sister who was supposed to protect her younger sister. Guilt and regret sometimes didn't have a logical reason.

Once in the spare room, they sat on the flowered bedspread together, cross-legged. "Where do things stand with you and Joe?" Beth asked, deciding not to beat around the bush.

"In limbo."

"Your fault or his?"

"Both, I guess. He hasn't called because he wants me to make up my mind and make our relationship official by getting engaged or moving in together. He doesn't see the problems. He thinks either of those would be a solution."

"Tell me again what you think the problems are," Beth suggested, hoping it might help her sister to list them.

"The big one is evident. Joe doesn't understand how an infant can turn your life upside down."

"The way Shara did yours?"

"Yes! Not that that's a bad thing. I'm not saying that. It's good. I can't wait to see Shara nursing her baby. I can't wait to hold her. But a new mom is sleep-deprived. A fussy baby affects everyone in the vicinity. A child is around-the-clock care. Shara's worried she can't do it, and I'm sure she can't do it alone. Mom and I will be there to help. But we're trying to work through all that too. Shara wants to be the mom. That means Mom and I have to back off at times and just let her struggle. But she doesn't realize how hard that struggle will be and neither does Joe. He wants to just step into the middle of all this."

"Did you ever think that maybe you should give him the chance to do that?"

"If I do, I know my responsibilities will split us up."

"But what's happening now, Clare? Aren't you being split up by the worry and the not knowing, and the thinking about everything that could go wrong?"

When tears flooded Clare's eyes, Beth moved over so she could put her arm around her. "Do you love Joe?"

"I do."

"Then why can't you let him help you work through this?"

"Because I don't want to fail. I don't want to fail as a mom to Shara, as a grandmom to the baby, or a partner for Joe."

"But if you don't give yourself a chance to succeed, how will you ever know you can?"

Tears ran down Clare's cheeks now, and she dug a tissue from her jeans pocket as if she'd done that a lot recently. "I guess I thought that if I just stood still and didn't make any decisions, I wouldn't lose him. But by not making any decisions I *am* losing him. What would *you* do?"

Beth seriously thought about it. "I'd call him and ask him to come over for dinner."

"But he said we needed space."

"Have you had space?"

"A week of it."

"All right. So what's the worst that can happen? He'd say *no*? He might say *yes*." As Sam had.

Clare studied her. "You know, *I* was the smart one when we were little. Now you seem to be the smart one."

Beth smiled. "I don't know how smart. I just try to look at both sides of everything. That's the way I've gotten through a lot of situations."

After Clare blew her nose, she said, "You and Sam look good together. There's a zing in the room when he's beside you."

"I'm not going to ask you to explain *zing*."

"But I will. It's chemistry. You make each other light up."

"And you feel lit up when Joe's around?" Beth changed the subject back to where it belonged.

"I do."

Beth gave a shrug and just arched her brows.

The doorbell gonged and Beth suddenly felt nervous. "That must be Gillian. She texted me when she landed. She's right on time."

Clare wanted to see Gillian. She did. They'd become friends after the search for Shara and they'd had phone conversations since. But right now she knew she had to call Joe.

As Beth headed for the doorway, Clare told her, "I'll be out soon, I promise," and took her phone from her pocket.

With a little wave Beth told her she understood.

Clare didn't know if Joe would be home or at the nursery. His professional life as a landscape architect kept him busy on weekends too. He had friends. He had buddies who'd been in the service. He watched over his dad. He could be with him this evening, watching replays of games on the sports channel.

Still, she dialed his number.

"Hi, Clare," he said. The uneasiness in his tone told her he didn't know what to expect with her call.

"I'm at Mom and Dad's."

"Is something wrong?"

"No. Mom made dinner. Beth and Sam are here and Gillian flew in."

He stayed silent and she didn't blame him. She'd left him out. One too many times? "Would you like to come join us? We won't be having dinner for at least a half hour yet."

"You don't want to be alone with me, do you?"

"That's not it at all. I miss you, Joe." Her voice cracked a bit. "I just had a talk with Beth, and she thinks I'm worrying too much about the future."

"There's a lot to worry about," he conceded.

"I know, and I've been trying to figure it all out. The problem is, I can't. No one could. Each day has to be lived before we can deal with the next one."

"So what are you saying?"

"I'm saying the only reason to be apart now is if we want to split up. I don't want that. I want to work out a life with you."

The sound of silence was disconcerting. Finally he responded, "But you want me to stop pushing for more than you can give. How do I know you'll eventually commit to me and a marriage? How do I know I'm not just spinning my wheels hoping for something that will never be?"

Joe had always been honest with her. Now she realized her lack of commitment had been his deepest concern. She had to tell him hers. "How do *I* know that if we move in together, when Shara and the baby are living with us, that a month into a situation with a baby not sleeping every night, *you* won't bail?" She never expected to have this conversation on the phone, but here it was, and she wasn't going to avoid it.

"Does that mean we're at a standstill?"

"Only if we want to be. Will you come to dinner? We can talk about this more tonight when we're alone."

He hesitated only a few moments and then he answered her. "Okay. I'll jump into the midst of whatever's happening tonight. Who knows what can happen when Gillian helps Beth. But you have to promise me you won't avoid a conversation later about our future."

"I promise."

"I'll be at your mom and dad's in fifteen minutes."

Relief washed over Clare as she said good-bye. She did love Joe. But did she have the courage to take a leap of faith and trust him?

Beth watched Gillian across the dinner table as she easily conversed with everyone sitting there. Somehow she managed to ignore the tension between Joe and Clare. Everyone could feel it. You didn't have to be psychic to know something was going on with them that they needed to resolve.

Her attention swiveled back to Gillian. This pretty woman could change her life. Gillian seemed normal in every way. But she wasn't normal because she had an unusual gift. From what Amanda had revealed, Beth knew that gift had sometimes been more of a burden than a joy.

Amanda asked Gillian, "So how are Nathan and Matthew?"

"Nathan has been particularly busy with new clients. Security, whether for businesses or private individuals, gets more technically complicated each day. Thank goodness he understands it because I don't. Maybe it's a guy-thing. Matthew surfs around on his tablet the same way Nathan does on his laptop. It takes me longer to get used to an app. Sometimes Jake's databases confuse the heck out of me when he's searching for something...or someone."

"He's using those to try to find Hannah, right?" Beth asked.

"He is, but it's slow going. I'm not sure it's any better than going into an historical center's archives and fumbling through file boxes. Yes, he can search. But if you don't have the right key word or the right name, it isn't much help. But, again, *he* knows exactly what he's doing."

"Are Nathan's girls with you often?" Amanda asked.

"They're with us at least one weekend a month, often more. At least a month in the summer. Nathan tries to keep up with what's going on with them at school and in sports. He sees them as often as he can and video-conferences with them. He doesn't feel uprooting them or having them switch houses often is beneficial to them."

"He's lucky to have an amicable relationship with his ex," Max said.

"It wasn't always that way. As you know, that's how I got involved in his life. But now both Nathan and Leona want what's best for the girls. If they get along and cooperate with each other, the girls will benefit."

Sam leaned close to Beth when he reached for a serving platter and murmured, "She seems normal in every way, doesn't she?"

Beth turned toward him, her cheek very close to his jaw. She took in a whiff of his aftershave and her pulse raced. "She is," she reminded him.

Sam just arched his brows in that way he had when he was skeptical. Whether he was skeptical or not, Beth was going to reserve judgment. She was hopeful about what Gillian could do.

After dessert and coffee, Amanda said to Beth, "It's almost seven. You and Gillian can use the spare room if you'd like."

Beth's therapist was supposed to be on call from seven to eight, just in case she needed her.

Standing beside Beth, Sam gently touched her arm. "Do you want me to come in with you?"

"I'd like that," Beth said.

However, Gillian overheard them. "It's probably better if Beth and I do this alone."

"You don't think Beth needs support?" Sam asked with a bit of sternness in his voice. Beth knew he was trying to protect her. Did he think Gillian had some nefarious motive in getting her alone? As if she wanted to hide something?

But Gillian didn't seem to mind his question. Instead she stepped closer to the two of them. "I don't know how to put this delicately," she said, "Except just to say it. There's energy between the two of you. Strong energy." She looked squarely at Sam. "I'm concerned if you're in the room with us, it's going to interfere with the process."

When he looked puzzled and even disbelieving, Gillian went on, "Think of electricity zipping back and forth in a wire between two posts. If someone comes along and cuts that wire, where does the energy go? It doesn't have a channel any more. It's striated and chaotic. I don't want that to happen to me and Beth."

"How long do you think this will take?" he asked.

Gillian shook her head. "There's no way of knowing. There's also no way of knowing whether we'll make any headway at all."

"But you want to make sure nothing distracts the process?" Sam asked, maybe beginning to understand.

"Yes."

As Sam studied Gillian and her steady gaze on him, he finally acquiesced. "All right. But I'll be right out here if you need me."

Beth took his hand and squeezed it because his support meant a lot. Then she and Gillian went to the spare room.

Chapter Eleven

Amanda's spare room was bright and sunny. It was decorated in yellow and blue. Two bedroom chairs at a small, marble-topped table were upholstered in a blue and white pin-striped fabric. The white iron bed wore a bedspread the same yellow and blue flowers as the curtains. The white-washed dresser looked like a refurbished antique as did the bowl and pitcher light on the nightstand.

"This room is so Amanda," Beth murmured.

"The Amanda you've come to know? Or the mom you've remembered?"

Beth gave Gillian a quick glance realizing she wasn't sure. "Now that you ask, I don't know. I know Amanda likes antiques, but the yellow and blue, and the flowers?" She shook her head. "Do three-year-olds really have memories?"

"Oh, they have memories. Whether they can access them or not is something different. Most of us can go back to being four or five years old and remember something impactful or emotional or fun."

Beth shook her head as she sat in one of the chairs. "Sometimes the sound of Max's laughter makes me think about being lifted up in his arms. Sometimes when Amanda's cooking, I have this fleeting picture of me standing on a chair beside her, watching. But there's nothing really recognizable or noteworthy."

Gillian sat across from Beth at the small table. "No memory of the police rescuing you at the mall?"

Beth understood that Gillian knew her whole story because Amanda had confided in her.

"No memory of the rescue per se. I do remember people milling about me at the mall and I was scared. I remember a tall bearded man who was bald looming over me, but I don't know if that memory is from the mall or from after I was kidnapped. It's sort of like if you put marbles in a jar and layer different colors, but then you shake the jar, the marbles go here, there and everywhere. All the colors mix up. That's the way my impressions and memories are."

Gillian glanced toward the door and the sound of voices outside. She'd shut it for privacy. She said, "I know there are a lot of people out there who really care about you."

"They do," Beth acknowledged.

"And you care about them."

"In different degrees," Beth said, wanting to be truthful. "Clare and I have a bond. I felt it from the first moment I saw her on that interview on TV. It just got stronger when we talked. She isn't just my sister, but she *feels* like my sister. And I like Joe. I can be around him without feeling some of the things I feel around other men."

"Can you explain that?"

"It's like I have this inside meter that tells me if I should be afraid of someone or not. Around some men, the hairs on the back of my neck might stand up, or I just have this overwhelming urge to back away. But Joe? He's okay. I think he's good for Clare and Shara."

"What's happening with you and Max and Amanda?"

"I feel like Amanda and I are becoming…friends. I know she wants to mother me. She wants to be my mother again. Once in a while when I'm around her, I almost feel that she is, or once was, my mother. But then I think about my adoptive mom and that confuses the issue. It's the same way with Max. Actually, I think he's keeping a distance on purpose. He didn't want to overwhelm me when we were all reunited and he told me that. He still doesn't want to. I know he worked a lot when I was a baby and we didn't spend much time together. Maybe that's why I don't feel what I do with Amanda. Is that possible?"

"Sure, it is. Do you feel you want to back away from him?"

"Oh, no. If nothing else, I feel safe around him. I know he'd never do anything to hurt me."

"That's a wonderful assurance to feel." Gillian let that idea sink in. "How about Shara?"

Beth couldn't help but smile. "She's impossible not to like. She feels like a younger sister. I worry about her and the baby and how that's all going to play out. Yet I also know with Amanda and Clare, and Max, on her side, she'll be okay."

"And then there's Sam."

Beth let out a breath. "You really feel something between us?"

"Loud and clear. And I'm pretty sure it's not just me. I noticed the looks Max and Amanda exchange when they see you and Sam talking or leaning close. You don't back away from him."

"No, I don't. I really like being with him. I really like—" She felt her face growing hot. "I like the idea of becoming more intimate with him. I'm scared, but I think I'm scared of the idea, not actually doing it. Do you know what I mean?"

"You're afraid because of your background you won't know how to react or you'll react badly?" Gillian asked.

"Exactly, and that's what scares me."

"You've explored this with your therapist."

"Not since Sam entered the picture."

"You might want to," Gillian requested.

"Or not. This feels like something that should just be private between me and him."

"You're going to have to follow your instincts on that."

"Yes, I am." So often Beth had learned that following her instincts was exactly what she needed to do.

"Do you think you're going to be able to forget about everybody who's out in the other room for a little while?"

Maybe that's why Gillian had wanted her to talk about all of them so the thoughts about them wouldn't be distracting her. "Yes, I can because I want to find Hannah."

"Do you have the button?"

Beth had wrapped the button in a piece of flannel. Now she took it from her jeans pocket and set it in the middle of the table.

Gillian directed, "Go ahead and unwrap it. Just let it sit there."

As Beth unwrapped the big red button, they both saw that there was a bit of red thread and a piece of wool fabric still attached to it.

Gillian directed her, "Take a few deep breaths."

Beth did, letting her hands rest on the table.

"Close your eyes and think about high school...and Hannah. What comes into your mind first?"

"Hannah stood up for me. Once we became friends, I didn't have to worry about kids making fun of me because of my scar...or my shyness. I didn't have to worry about anything when she was with me."

"Sort of like a sister."

Beth nodded. "Exactly like that. We shared like sisters. I told her my fears. She talked about the kind of family she'd like to adopt her."

"What kind of family did she want?"

"A mom who cooked and a dad who'd played video games. And I..." Suddenly an image wisped just out of her reach. Not about Hannah, though. It was Max. Could she remember him playing tag with her? With her and Clare? The image reappeared and she heard his laugh, felt the wind in her hair. She smelled the grass as she took a tumble and her dad tickled her. She giggled.

"Beth?"

"I think I just had a memory of Max."

"Can you stay in the memory?"

Beth tried to picture the scene again. But she couldn't. She shook her head. "It's gone."

Gillian waited a few moments. "Let's go back to your memories about Hannah. Can you describe her to me?"

Memories of Hannah came easily. "She always told me she was interesting looking but not pretty. But I thought she was pretty. She had big green eyes that got even bigger when she was excited about something. Her hair was dark brown, the color of dark chocolate. She always said her hair was her best feature because it was thick and wavy."

"Was she as tall as you or shorter than you?"

"Why do you need to know that?"

"If Jake finds someone, he has to compare statistics. Height would help along with hair and eye color."

Beth thought about it. "She was shorter than me and thinner than me, maybe by a couple of inches and five to ten pounds. Gillian, I don't know why, but my memories of her seem more vivid right now. Do you think that's because I'm searching?"

"I'm not sure. It could be that, or … You've had this feeling for a couple of months, right?"

Beth nodded. "Even before we started the search. Not like she's trying to connect with me but like I'm connected with her."

"Maybe she's in need of a friend right now, or going through a difficult time of her life."

"So this is even more important."

"Try not to think about the importance, just the connection. The fact that your memories are vivid could help. I'm going to pick up the button and hold onto it and just see if I get any sensations from it, okay?"

Beth nodded, practically holding her breath.

However, Gillian suggested, "Breathe, Beth. Just breathe. Anxiety, panic, confusion and worry block energy channels."

So Beth thought of Hannah as she remembered her— the last time they'd walked around the yard at the group home, the last time they'd enjoyed dinner at Beth's home.

Gillian lifted the button and set it in her palm. Then she closed her eyes. It seemed like a really long time passed and Beth was sure nothing good was going to happen. Yet she kept her focus on the picture of Hannah in her mind, her green eyes, her wide smile.

"Did Hannah like the beach?"

"The beach?"

"I'm getting an impression of the word 'tide' that has waves with it. And of a giant statue of Neptune."

Sifting through her memories, Beth said, "Hannah mentioned taking a vacation once before her mom got sick. I think they went to the ocean for a weekend. She said it was the only vacation they'd ever had."

"Do you have any idea where she lived before she came to the group home?"

"I think they lived in Monroeville."

"Did she have a black eye at any time when you knew her?"

Beth thought about it. "She could be uncooperative. She was rebellious and not the housemom's favorite. But I don't remember a black eye. In fact, she could usually get the better of anyone who tried to hurt her. What are you seeing, Gillian?"

"You have to understand something, Beth. When I receive sensations, they aren't necessarily on a continual time line. Events can come to me, but they're all mixed up. So I don't know what's in the past and what's in the present." Gillian closed her eyes again and asked, "Did she like boats?"

"I don't remember anything about boats."

Gillian closed her hand over the button, fingering the wool fabric still attached. "I'm seeing a pier, you know the kind of place where people fish. And I'm not sure—" She stopped.

"Not sure about what?" Beth didn't know whether to prod her or to keep silent.

"Starfish Road."

"That's where Hannah is?"

"Not necessarily, but it could be someplace she's been. There are many years to cover, and there's no assurance that what I'm seeing is in the present."

"So what do we do?"

Gillian held up her hand and Beth became quiet. Minutes dragged by. Beth became distracted by noises outside of the spare bedroom.

Gillian still had her eyes closed. Her face was relaxed, but Beth could tell she was intent on something by the squareness of her shoulders.

Finally Gillian opened her eyes. She set the button down on the flannel once more. "I'm going to call Jake and tell him everything that came to me. He's good at putting clues together."

"Did you tell me everything that came to you?"

Gillian looked her straight in the eye. "No."

"I don't understand."

"Beth, sometimes I can't put sensations into words. I

don't want to worry you or get your hopes up too high. So let's just see what Jake comes up with."

Beth had been around therapists and counselors and advocates long enough that she suspected what Gillian wasn't telling her. "It's the black eye, isn't it? You think it's in the present."

"I don't know. Let's see what Jake ferrets out."

Beth wanted answers and she wanted them now. But she knew she'd have to wait…and pray that Hannah was alive and safe and well.

Chapter Twelve

On the drive home that night, Sam was quiet and Beth was too. *He* was quiet because he didn't know what to say. After watching Beth and Gillian become closeted in the spare bedroom—and it had seemed like a hugely long time they were in there--they'd emerged. They'd both explained some of what had happened. He'd suspected they'd both kept details to themselves. He didn't know what to think about any of it.

However, he did know one thing. He wanted to support Beth in whatever happened. He didn't just feel protective of her, he felt so much more. He still didn't know where they were going with this relationship. Did he really want to get more involved when he'd be leaving the country again?

Yet the more time he spent with Beth, the more time he wanted to spend with her. After he parked at *Yesteryear's Treasures*, he asked, "Do you want me to come up with you?"

"Yes," she said without hesitation.

After they mounted the steps and went inside the apartment, she looked around the kitchen. "My thoughts are in a jumble and I'd like to sort them out. Would you like something to drink?"

Crossing to her, he took her by the elbows. "You don't have to treat me like a guest."

"But you are, aren't you?" She pulled away and shook her head. "I'm sorry. I don't know what I'm saying. I'm a bit confused."

If she wanted to pull away, he had to let her. But if she didn't want to pull away—

Taking her hand, he led her into the living room. "Let's talk."

"I don't know if it will help." She sank down onto the sofa. "I don't even know why I asked you to come up."

He lowered himself next to her. "Maybe because you just want to *be* with me."

"Being with you can take on many forms," she said with a small smile. "Some of those forms could confuse me more than I already am."

He laid his hand on her cheek for a moment and then slid his fingers under her hair. There was an attraction between them that was too strong to ignore. "I've wanted to kiss you all evening, but I know your mind is some-where else...and on someone else. Tell me about your experience with Gillian, what it felt like."

"That's simple. It felt like I was on a roller coaster ride. We talked a bit first about everybody who was in the living room. I think Gillian did that so I wouldn't be distracted by voices if I heard them coming from there."

"Talked about us?" he asked with a quirked brow.

"Yes, my connection to each person, and how I felt about them."

He couldn't help himself. He asked, "And what did you say about me?"

"I said I liked being with you."

He nodded. "And Gillian felt the energy between us?"

"She did. It makes you wonder, doesn't it? If people can see it."

He chuckled. "We could take a poll the next time we go into a restaurant."

She playfully socked his arm with her fist. And then she became serious again. "I never know if there's going to be a next time with you. If this is something that's going to last."

"I don't know that either, Beth."

She sighed. "After our initial conversation, Gillian moved on to Hannah and my memories about her. I remembered things I thought I'd forgotten. I think Gillian was trying to make my connection to Hannah stronger. That would help when the button came into play."

"So tell me what happened when Gillian picked up the button."

"At first she just held it, and then she began asking me questions—if Hannah had liked the ocean. She kept getting that tide impression, as we mentioned, but she knew it was spelled T-I-D-E. She said something about a Neptune statue. Then she asked me if Hannah liked boats."

"Did she?"

"I don't know," Beth admitted.

"Anything else?" he prompted, getting the feeling Beth was holding something back.

Beth glanced away then met his gaze once more. "Gillian asked me if Hannah had ever had a black eye."

"Why do you think she asked that?"

"I don't know. I don't know what she was seeing or feeling. I told her I didn't remember Hannah ever having a black eye, not when I knew her. After that Gillian explained that when she gets impressions, time isn't always on a logical continuum. Sometimes she can't tell if something is from the past or the present."

"That could be a way out, so if she's wrong, what she says would still make sense."

"Are you still skeptical?" She moved away from him a few inches, as if his skepticism was a wall between them.

"Beth, you're counting on this woman's impressions. This whole situation is so out of the ordinary. Do you really believe in a reading like that, or do you just *want* to believe?"

"I don't like you using that term *reading* as if she's some kind of fake psychic. She's not. She's found missing persons. She's found lost children. She's even helped the police departments. Do you think they'd rely on her if she was fake?"

Sam ran his hand through his hair. "You want me to tell you I believe as much as you do. I can't do that. But I can tell you this. If Gillian's partner turns up anything from her clues about where Hannah Miller is, I will support you in whatever you want to do. If you want to track her down, I'll go with you."

"How can you do that with your schedule?"

"I'll manage it somehow. We'll figure it out together. If Gillian's partner, this Jake Donovan, turns up nothing or can't make any connections with her clues, I don't want you to be heartbroken."

"I can't tell you I won't be. But I do know one thing. I feel as if Hannah needs me, the same way I needed her all of those years ago when she took me under her wing."

Sam could see Beth believed what she was saying with all of her heart. "Maybe *I'm* the one who's not normal," he decided. "Maybe *I'm* the one who can't feel connections."

Beth swiftly protested, "That's not true or you wouldn't be here with me. Maybe you should talk to Max. He was like you. He didn't believe in Gillian either. But then out in New Mexico, when she met him and Amanda there to find Shara, it was because of her that they did. They did some PI and surveillance work with her, but it was because of her direction, her sensations and impressions that they knew where to go. Max is a believer now too. I think in some ways, Gillian restored his hope in life again—the basic idea that good things can happen."

With a furrowed brow, Sam said, "I knew him before Shara ran away, and before you came back into his life. All those years, he'd acted like a man who'd lost everything but was going on anyway. Now he's changed. There *is* hope in him again. I attributed that to you coming back."

"It was everything and how it all worked together," she insisted.

"Do you believe fate brought you to my practice?"

"Fate and your résumé," she teased.

"Here I thought we were delving into the realm of karma."

"Your karma brought me to you," she murmured, looking at him as if that were a very good thing.

He encircled her with his arms and lifted her chin up with his thumb. He didn't have to say what he wanted because Beth leaned close to him. Their kiss was as natural as breathing though they lost their breath over it.

After he ended the kiss, she took a deep breath and smiled. "One of these nights when you kiss me, I'll ask you to stay the night."

When she said those words, he knew she wasn't teasing him. She was being honest. "You're considering all that staying-the-night would mean." He was too. "You'll have to be ready."

"I will be."

How he hoped that was so.

***

Ever since Shara had made that emergency department visit, Clare wouldn't leave her by herself. However, tonight, she and Joe did need privacy.

After Clare and Shara drove home and went inside, Shara asked her mom, "Are you and Joe going to talk?"

"Joe just went home to change and to catch up on calls. Then he'll be back over."

"Why don't you just go over to his house?" Shara asked.

"Because I don't want to leave you here by yourself."

"Mom, I'm not a baby. I have a cell phone and so do you. Go over to Joe's and talk to him. Didn't you tell me communication is everything?"

When Clare looked at her daughter she could easily see that Shara didn't want to be guarded twenty-four hours a day. She needed space just like anyone did. Although Clare was worried about her, she couldn't let that worry dictate all of her actions.

"What are *you* going to do?" she asked her daughter.

"I'm going to settle in bed with my laptop. I have assignments due tomorrow and I want to go over them one last time before I send them in. Really, Mom, I'll be fine for a couple of hours, or for however long it takes for you to patch things up with Joe."

"How do you know we're going to be able to patch things up?"

"Because you love him."

The sudden silence between them seemed to make Shara's words echo. But Clare didn't duck from that echo. She did love Joe, and she'd never told him.

"Even if I love him, that doesn't mean we can make things work."

"Don't use me as an excuse," Shara warned her.

"You'd never be an excuse. You're part of my life—a main part. I want you to be happy in whatever decision I make. It all just seems so complicated."

Shara eyed her steadily. "Go to him, Mom," she said again. "You know you want to." She took her cell phone from her pocket. "I promise this will be right beside my fingers the whole time you're gone. If I even have a little cramp, I'll text or phone you. I promise."

"All right," Clare finally agreed with a smile, giving her daughter a tight hug. "But I'll probably meet him in his carport if he's on his way over here."

"If you do, you can do it right there," Shara said irreverently.

"Shara!"

"You think I don't know the two of you have sex?"

"I'm not discussing this with you. I'll text you before I come back home so you'll know it's me opening the door." Clare picked up her purse with her phone, grabbed her sweater, and hurried out the back door.

She jogged across the yard toward Joe's side porch. Her shoes ruffled the grass as she hurried, not knowing if she was headed for a beginning or an ending. She was nervous and had been all evening because she'd known this confrontation was coming. She'd tried to concentrate on Beth and her sister finding Hannah. It seemed as if Gillian had come through again. Now it was her partner Jake Donovan's turn to do his thing. But all Clare could think about for the most part was this talk with Joe, and the problems that didn't seem to have enough solutions.

At his kitchen door, she knocked and then pushed it open. Since they had been dating, they had keys to each other's houses and they had never stood on formality. She found Joe right there in the kitchen hunched over the counter. His cell phone was at his ear and he was typing onto his electronic tablet. He looked up when she walked in and he mouthed, "Client."

Joe had become involved in landscaping for a model home project lately and it was taking up many of his waking hours. Clients wanted what they wanted when they wanted it. She went into his living room to wait.

Although she went over her situation with Joe again and again in her mind, she couldn't seem to come up with a solution. Her house wasn't big enough for him to move into. Not really. Not without them bumping into each other every time they turned around. And Shara was going to need privacy. After the baby was born, the lack of space would be even more noticeable. On the other hand, Joe's house... Would he want it invaded by two women and a baby? He didn't have that much more room than she did. The whole thing just seemed impossible.

She felt tears burn in her eyes because she *did* love Joe. The timing just seemed wrong. She could lose him because she couldn't give their relationship her full attention. That's what she had to explain to him and make him understand.

A few minutes later he joined her in the living room. He could see she was upset. Sitting beside her, he asked, "What's wrong? Are you breaking up with me?"

"No. I mean that's not what I want." The catch in her voice told it all. "But I can't give you or our relationship the attention it needs right now. I don't know what to do about that. It's not going to get any better after Shara's baby is born."

Joe didn't touch her. He looked straight ahead for a few moments. He clasped his hands and dropped them between his knees. "What if I tell you that I have a solution, but you're going to have to trust me big time to jump into it." Now he did turn and look at her.

"You're going to clone me?" She tried to joke but it fell flat.

"If I could, I would, but then one of you would miss out on all the family stuff you're into. I want you to think about something. Do you know how long it's been since I had anybody but my dad as family? Do you realize that I *want* a family?"

"A ready-made one?"

He shrugged. "It seems to me that would be a jump start. Do you want to hear what I'm thinking?"

"I do." Hearing about what he was thinking was so much better than fighting.

"Here goes. I discussed this with my father."

Clare had visited Joe's dad with him. They'd had dinner there several times. She liked his father. He'd had some orthopedic problems lately and she knew Joe was worried about that.

"Did you need a sounding board?" For her, talking with her sister had helped.

"My dad could always be a sounding board but our discussion was more than that. My father is older than your parents, sixty-eight next year. He has back and knee issues but he's been fighting them for years. I'll probably be taking over the business soon and he'll come in and work whenever he wants to."

She nodded, having no idea where this was going.

"I grew up in the house where he lives and there are still memories of my mother there. That's why he hasn't wanted to think about moving. One of his big problems is that he doesn't like accepting help. I offered to move in with him when I came back from Afghanistan but he'd have none of that. He still doesn't want it. So I suggested an alternative. I can sell my house and buy his. That would give him enough money to move into a maintenance-free condo or a retirement center."

"Would he agree to that?"

"He's considering it."

"How does this affect us?"

"You've seen my dad's house. It's a Cape Cod with a master suite downstairs and two bedrooms upstairs. It's not huge but it's more space than either you or I have now. Would you consider selling your house and moving in there with me? We could renovate it a bit, whatever you and Shara would like. You and I would take the downstairs bedroom and Shara could have the upstairs. She could have a bedroom and use the other room as a nursery, or if she wants to keep the baby in her room with her, she could use the other room as a sitting area with a TV or whatever she'd like. I'm not asking you again to marry me...because I know you wouldn't accept. You're afraid I can't handle taking on a teenage daughter and her baby. This plan would give you a cushion in lots of ways. You'd have the money from the sale of your house to use for another place if we didn't work out. I don't like the idea of giving myself a loophole but I also believe that's the security you need to move forward. Am I right?"

Joe's plan was huge and life changing for all of them. Her head spun with the thought of it. She'd never imagined doing anything like this. But it did make sense. Neither of them would be losing anything. Joe would have his childhood home, and she and Shara could just live day by day and see if it all worked out.

"Joe, I can't believe you and your dad are willing to do this."

"Dad knows this move would be the best thing for him, especially if he wants to remain independent. He can't do the stairs at the house any more, not without a lot of pain.

And if he can't do them, the upstairs space isn't being used. I wanted to bring a cleaning lady in but he didn't want the invasion. A condo would be easier for him to take care of. I know you need to think about this. It's a big decision. But tell me how you're feeling at this moment."

"Overwhelmed, but in a good way. I can't give you an answer this minute, not because of me, but because of Shara. I want to talk to her about it. I have to consider her needs and her happiness too, as well as the baby's. I do think this would work if she wants to give it a try. I'll be there to help her. Mom has said she'll babysit whenever we need her. Still, do you know what you're taking on?"

"Let's see," he said. "I'd have a life partner I love. I'd have a daughter if she wants to think of me as a dad. And I'd have a baby to practice with if we'd want to have or adopt one of our own."

"I'm not getting any younger," Clare reminded him.

"That's something we can discuss once we've committed to this idea after Shara's baby's born. So you're really open to it?"

"I am." Clare knew her voice sounded as excited as she felt. Taking his hand, she interlaced her fingers with his. "I should have said how I'm feeling before now. I've been afraid of so many things. But I want a life with you, Joe, I do. I *do* love you."

He took her in his arms then and kissed her with a fervor that told her he wanted the same thing. Breaking off the kiss, he asked in a gravelly voice, "Can you stay?"

"Shara thinks I should stay and make love with you. She has a cell phone by her side."

He leaned back and laughed. "She actually said that?"

"Actually, she said we should meet in your carport and do it there."

He laughed again, stood, took her hand, and led her to his bedroom.

Chapter Thirteen

Beth was having lunch with Sam on Monday when she received a phone call. She and Sam had spent yesterday together—talking, kissing, laughing. They'd watched a movie in the afternoon and fallen asleep on Sam's couch together. It had seemed so natural. After they'd awakened from their nap, they'd driven to Harrisburg for dinner. When he'd left her at her apartment last night, she hadn't wanted him to go. Yet she was still hesitant to ask him to stay.

This morning Sam had had several surgeries. But they'd made plans to catch a quick bite at a restaurant near the hospital before he returned to his office for appointments.

Normally Beth let her calls roll to voicemail when she was with Sam, but she'd been on pins and needles ever since her session with Gillian on Saturday.

When her phone played, she glanced at Sam. He said, "Take it. I know you want to see who's calling."

After she checked the screen, she said breathlessly,

"It's Gillian." She'd flown home yesterday after spending the night at Amanda's and Max's house.

Sam stopped eating and listened to Beth's end of the conversation.

Gillian said, "Jake believes we found Hannah."

"And what do *you* think?" Beth asked.

"I agree that everything fits."

"Where is she?" Beth couldn't seem to wait for the answers.

"She's living in Virginia Beach. From what Jake could find out, she works at a marina there, *Fit To Be Tide*."

"Tide." Beth remembered what Gillian had told her, and the impression she had gotten.

"Yes, in more ways than one. Tide is in the title of the marina and the tide comes in at the beach. A giant statue of Neptune is located on the boardwalk there."

"Hannah's name is the same?"

"Yes. Jake finally connected with a retired group home counselor who remembered Hannah. He connected Jake with a woman who volunteered at the Pennsylvania Partners Group Home in Scranton, the facility she'd been transferred to. She was there until she turned seventeen. They found a foster family to take her in, but she ran away from there."

"Tracing records from Virginia Beach back," Gillian continued, "Jake found out that at eighteen Hannah bought a used car in Scranton. After that, she headed for Virginia Beach. She's worked at the marina for years."

"I wonder why she never tried to contact me."

"When I felt impressions about her, I got the feeling that she felt insecure. Could she have blamed herself for what happened to you?"

Beth considered that. "Possibly. Do you have an address where she lives?"

"Not exactly. Jake accessed her cell phone records. He had an address for six months ago, but she discontinued her cell service then. At least she did on *that* phone or with *that* service."

"But you're sure she's still in Virginia Beach?"

"Yes. Jake is certain she's still working at the marina. He called there and fished around. He pretended he was interested in a charter. She gave her name when she answered the phone."

"Does she know I'm looking for her?"

"No. Jake didn't tell her any of that. He simply pretended to be a customer. He didn't want to spook her."

"So why do you think he can't find an address for her?"

"I'm getting a feeling about that. I think she could be living with someone, or maybe she moved in with friends. Maybe she's splitting the rent and her name isn't on the lease."

Something in Gillian's voice alerted Beth. "You have an inkling about what's going on, don't you?"

"When I held the button your mom kept, I could sense she was tied to someone. Beth, I want you to be careful."

"Why?"

"You don't know who Hannah has become. You also don't know who her friends are now. You don't know the person she could be living with."

"What makes you think I should be careful?"

"I listened in on Jake's call to Hannah. From her voice

and her spirit, I can tell she's happy working at the marina, and I got the sense that she does love the beach and boating."

"I hear a *but* coming."

"I don't think she's happy with her personal life."

"You mean the person she's living with?"

"I'm not sure about that, Beth. I just know that I see something dark around her."

"Something dark. I understand that. I lived with it for months." Beth suddenly realized what she'd said. Before now she'd had no feelings or memories about her time when Luther Brown had kept her a prisoner.

"Beth, are you okay?"

"I don't know. I was indifferent to those months with my kidnapper before. I thought I was just too young to remember. I didn't see them as light or dark. They were just something grey and blank."

"And now?"

"Now I...I suddenly get the chills when I think about them. I don't want to think about them."

"I'm not a counselor, Beth," Gillian reminded her. "You need to call yours. But I will tell you this. You have two choices. You can either try to block those memories, or go on with what you're doing. You can stop or you can let them come in. In the long run, you know that's the better way."

"In the long run, what are they going to do to me?"

"You're a strong enough woman to deal with whatever they are. You have a support system around you. You not only have your adoptive family, but your original family. And now you have Sam, too."

Beth lowered her voice. "I don't want to mix him up in any drama."

"Talk to him, Beth. What do you think you're going to do?"

"I'm going to go to that marina and maybe even charter a boat."

"Don't go alone."

"I have lots of possibilities. Amanda or Max might go with me."

"Do you want me to join you there?"

"That's not necessary."

"If you drive to Virginia Beach and you hit a dead end, or you think you need me there, call me. I'll fly in. I was helpful to Max and Amanda when they were looking for Shara. We had no idea where she was in Albuquerque. But you do have an idea where Hannah is in Virginia Beach."

"You'd really fly down there?"

"I would. And if I could, I'd bring Nathan and Matthew. We could show them an east coast beach. Do you want me to meet you there?"

"I don't know. I need time to talk this over with someone. I'll call you back in a couple of hours, okay?"

"That's fine. I always have my cell with me."

After Beth ended the call, Sam asked her, "Good news?"

"Yes. Gillian knows where Hannah works. It's at a marina in Virginia Beach."

Sam thought about it. "So what's happening next?"

"That's what I'm trying to decide. Gillian said she could meet me there."

"Do you need Gillian if you know where Hannah works?"

"But I don't know where she *lives*."

"Virginia Beach is only about four and half hours away. When do you want to go?"

"As soon as I can. I feel an urgency about this."

"I have appointments this afternoon and surgeries for most of tomorrow. But I have the day free on Wednesday and I can find somebody to cover appointments for me on Thursday."

"Are you saying you'd go along with me?"

"Do you want a road trip buddy?"

"Of course, I do...if it's *you*."

He reached over and took her hand, caressing her palm with his thumb. "Maybe we can do this without Gillian. If we don't get anywhere, then you can call her and she can meet you there."

"That sounds like a plan."

"Gillian is sure this is *your* Hannah Miller?"

"As sure as she can be, at least for now."

"Are you prepared for a dead end, or the wrong Hannah Miller?"

"Have a little faith, Sam. I trust Gillian." But she could still see he didn't have much faith in Gillian's gift. She just hoped she could prove him wrong.

Thinking about Beth, what she meant to him and what he was going to do about it, absorbed much of Sam's off-work time. When he closed his eyes, he saw her face.

When they didn't have a date, he wished they did. When he thought about driving her to Virginia Beach, he was concerned for her.

Working on patient records on the computer at his desk the following evening, he leaned back in his chair and thought again about what the trip meant to her. Apparently Beth hadn't had many friends over her life. Because she was afraid to get close? Because she could be shy and didn't like to take the first step? Because she'd been bullied? Because she'd felt different and acted different from most other children?

Considering what she'd told him about her relationship with Hannah, Hannah had been her first real friend. During the teenage years, that mattered so much. Maybe even more for a girl than for a guy—to be able to talk about feelings, boys, school, dating, teachers, even parents. It was so important at that age.

Although he'd had a horrific home life, he'd had sports, he'd had teammates, he'd had a couple of work friends he could talk to. No, not about the abuse, but about guy stuff. That had kept him sane. So had his school work because it had given him the motivation about the future, even though he hadn't known exactly what that future would bring. He'd just known he was going to have a better future than his parents had. He was going to be someone, do something important, somehow stand up for kids who had no one to stand up for them.

Beth's parents had been overprotective and who could blame them? After all, from what they knew, she'd been abandoned in a mall. No one had claimed her. That had certainly been grounds for overprotectiveness. On his part, he'd had no protection. In some ways they were so different. Yet in other ways...they connected on a level so deep he couldn't even reach it. And since he'd met Beth, she'd reminded him of a butterfly breaking out of a chrysalis.

When his phone buzzed, he turned away from the computer and picked up the handset.

"I knew you'd still be at your office" a familiar voice said.

Sam smiled when he heard Cole Prescott's voice. Cole was the director of Kids Cause and stationed in New York.

Sam had been working with him for years. Cole had had his start in trauma medicine and was a few years older than Sam. He was usually too busy to call for just a friendly chat, so Sam suspected this was something important. "What can I do for you?"

"That's not the question. The question is what can *you* do for *me?*" Cole said tongue in cheek with a smile in his voice.

Sam had to laugh. "Okay. What can *I* do for *you?*"

"Joking aside," Cole said, "I need you in Africa two weeks earlier than we'd planned. Is that possible?"

Sam studied his desk calendar. He still wasn't crazy about the computer version. He liked to see the dates right in front of his nose, on the desk where he could contemplate them. Two weeks earlier than planned was only about two weeks away. He'd been thinking about this trip a lot. Not because of the work itself, but because of Beth.

"I thought you'd jump at the chance," Cole said when Sam didn't respond.

"I've met someone," he said honestly.

"Whoa! That's unexpected."

"I'm not sure that's a compliment."

"It has nothing to do with being a compliment or not. You've always put work first. You've always put Kids Cause first."

That was certainly true. "I'd like to see where this goes. Being away for six weeks could finish it before it starts."

"You're serious?"

"I usually am."

He heard a resigned sigh coming from Cole. "Like I said, I never expected this. I could fish around for someone else—" He let his voice trail off. "If that's what you want."

Did he want that? Was he willing to put Beth before his work with Kids Cause?

"Do you like the website?" Sam asked.

"Yeah, I like the website. I told you I did when I approved it. What does that have to do with this?"

"The woman I'm dating—she's the one who designed it."

There was a long pause. "She obviously likes kids. And since she did it for free, she obviously wants to help the cause. Am I headed in the right direction?"

"Maybe. I didn't even think about it...consciously. But maybe my subconscious was wondering if she'd like to be a volunteer and go along."

"You know the requirements—she has to have a passport. She has to have vaccinations and she'd need a few days of training."

"I know. Are you open to it?"

"How old is she?"

"She's thirty."

"Mature?"

"In most ways. She's been through trauma herself. I know she'd be compassionate and caring with any kids who need help."

"Do I hear a *but*?"

"I don't know."

"Let me help with part of your dilemma. I'd be open to the possibility. But I'm going to need to know soon...about both of you."

"Within a week?"

"A week at the latest."

"I'll talk to her and then get back to you."

"You know volunteers are hard to find. I'd be grateful for a good one. So good luck."

When Sam hung up the receiver, he knew he was going to need it.

On Wednesday, Beth glanced at Sam often on the drive to Virginia Beach. Although they talked on and off, he seemed distracted. It was just a feeling she got but she had Hannah on her mind. What was she going to say and do if she found her? How would Hannah feel about Beth putting a private investigator on her trail...or a psychic?

She skittered around that thought until they arrived at their destination. Sam had made reservations for them at the *Seaside View*, a beach-side hotel. The location was a ten minute drive from the marina and there was a fishing pier near the marina. Gillian had been right about that too.

When she and Sam stepped into the lobby of the hotel, she spotted a restaurant that looked like a nice one.

At the check-in desk, the clerk said to Sam, "I see that you asked for adjoining rooms but we don't have any of those available. How about a suite? We'll charge the same price for the suite as the two adjoining rooms. There *are* two bedrooms in the suites."

Beth jumped in. "We don't need a suite. A regular room is fine with me."

But Sam put his hand on her shoulder and said to the clerk, "Give us a minute." In a lowered voice he said to Beth, "I'd like to be closer than in a room next door with no adjoining door. What about you?"

"You have something on your mind," and she knew it wasn't just making out...or more.

He looked disgruntled for a moment but then he reminded her, "If we find Hannah, or if we don't find Hannah, it could dig up memories for you. I don't like the idea of you being locked in a room by yourself. Do you want to be completely alone like that?"

She had one thing on her mind and one thing only—finding Hannah. All she wanted to do was climb back in Sam's SUV and see if their lead panned out. She hadn't really thought about all the rest. Sam could be right, of course. She was used to being alone, but should she be by herself in these circumstances?

"I'm paying for half the suite," she insisted.

"Beth—"

"It's the only way I'll agree."

"That's an ultimatum."

"Those are my terms. I didn't agree for you to come along so you could pay my way."

"If your mother had come along and wanted a suite, would you be arguing with her?"

"That's different."

He arched his brows.

"It is, Sam, and you know it."

He gave her another look that said he didn't like her terms. Suddenly an idea popped into her head that she didn't approve of at all. "Did Max ask you to watch over me? Because if *that's* the reason you want a suite, we *will* be staying in separate rooms."

Sam ran his hand through his hair and she noticed he did that when he was frustrated or stumped. He looked torn. He pulled her another foot away from the registration desk then held her by the shoulders. "I care about you. *That's* why I came along. But I will tell you Max gave me a call and he asked me to keep you safe. There's nothing wrong with that, Beth. He's acting like a father would. I am acting like a boyfriend. I don't want you to confuse the two."

One look into Sam's eyes and she could see that he meant it. Thinking about his kisses, she easily said, "I won't confuse the two. Believe me, I think about you and Max in entirely different lights."

A smile broke across Sam's lips. "So we're good on the suite?"

"We're good on the suite."

Fifteen minutes later, after the bellboy let them into their accommodations, Beth looked around. While he was putting their suitcases in their bedrooms, she noticed the flat screen TV, the love seat and sofa, the small dining table that would seat four in the common area. The galley kitchen was large enough and equipped sufficiently to cook a meal.

As Sam tipped the bellboy, she went down the hall to examine the two separate bedrooms. Her suitcase was on the bed in a room decorated in blues. From the muted contemporary artwork above the bed, to the draperies with their white sheers underneath, it was a pleasant room and looked comfortable. She peeked into the bedroom next door and saw that Sam had the same king-sized bed, the same dresser, but his room was decorated in hues of green.

After she returned to the living room, she found him pulling two bottles of water from the refrigerator. He held one out to her.

She took it from him, twisted off the top, and drank a few swallows. He did the same. He was dressed casually today in a sage green polo shirt and khakis with Docksides on his feet. He looked as if he belonged here at a beach resort. However, she realized that Sam fit in anywhere. She had worn jeans and a blue plaid cotton shirt. The outfit was comfortable for traveling. Sneakers had seemed advisable since they were going to visit a marina.

"Do you want to get some lunch?" he asked. "Or go to the marina?"

"The marina."

"No surprise there."

Suddenly she asked Sam, "What if Hannah doesn't want to see me? What if she wishes I never found her? Maybe she doesn't want any of those old memories cropping back up. Maybe that's why she never contacted me."

He deliberately set down his bottle of water on the counter then crossed to her slowly. As he wrapped his arms around her, he advised her, "Don't push yourself into panic. You can't predict what's going to happen in this situation, Beth. You can't."

"You want me to roll with the punches."

"I want you to focus on the moment."

"With you or with Hannah?"

"Both." He tipped her chin up and kissed her.

Whether it was to help her focus on the moment, or to distract her, she wasn't sure. But it certainly did both.

In a way, the water called to Beth. Maybe it wasn't the ocean as much as the waves on the beach.

As Sam parked in the paved lot near the marina, she said, "One of my most vivid memories is of a vacation Max and Amanda, Clare and I took to the beach. I guess Hannah and I had that favorite memory in common. Clare and I built sand castles all day. Mom..." She stopped, realizing what she'd said. "Amanda kept slathering us with sunscreen. Most of all, I remember simply sitting on the beach with Clare, staring out at the ocean. Clare whispered something in my ear."

"Do you remember what it was?"

"Probably a childhood secret. Or else she was telling me a story about mermaids living in the ocean. When I saw Clare on that TV interview that she did with Shara and Max and Amanda, and I realized how much she looked like me, that beach memory popped up. I don't understand why others won't."

"You were so young. It's not unusual for a three or four year old not to have any memories from back then. You remember that memory with Clare because it was a happy memory and you loved her dearly. Do you realize that by going back to that memory, you just called Amanda *Mom?*"

"I felt it for a moment."

He reached over and squeezed her hand. "You remembered Amanda slathering you with suntan lotion because she cared about you, and you could feel it probably in each stroke. That's a muscle memory along with a mind memory."

"It's a shame we can't click a button like we do on the computer and save the memories we want and delete the other ones."

"Now that's a subject for a neuroscientist."

She smiled. "Maybe so."

After they climbed out of the SUV, they spotted the marina office. There were boats everywhere. Sam pointed to one with a pilothouse. "There's a fortune's worth of boats here."

"I have no idea how much any of them are worth," Beth said.

He waved toward the sleek white boat with the pilothouse. "That one looks to be about twenty years old.

If you wanted to buy it, I think you'd have to put out about three hundred fifty thousand dollars."

Beth whistled. "Oh, my gosh."

"It isn't just the boat but the upkeep too," he elaborated. Pointing to a much smaller boat, he explained, "That's about a thirty-one foot cruiser, possibly around ten years old. It's hard to tell, but something like that is worth about seventy thousand dollars."

"How do you know boats?"

"I deal with a lot of fund raising. That also means dealing with very wealthy donors. I've been out on several boats, talking about what I do and Kids Cause."

"Your world is so much broader than mine."

"There's nothing stopping you from broadening yours."

Only my fear, Beth thought. It was a fear of doing anything new, anything that was a risk, anything that wasn't practical, anything she couldn't control. She felt so out of control in this relationship with Sam. Because it was new and a risk? Absolutely.

Trying not to think about what they would find in the marina, she concentrated on the steps leading up to the one story building. "I'm nervous," she whispered.

"She was your best friend."

Normally he would have opened the door for her. That was just the kind of man Sam was. But this time, Beth stepped in front of him, took her courage in her hands, and gripped the door handle.

He nodded, seeming to understand that she had to go first. She had to open the door herself either to end an old chapter of her life, or begin a new one.

Beth yanked open the door and stepped over the threshold. When she did, her gaze went to the desk where charters were scheduled and boats rented. The receptionist was talking on the phone. Beth stared at the woman who was sitting there, feeling shock.

If nothing else proved Gillian's gift was real, this did.

Chapter Fourteen

Beth restrained a gasp, at least she hoped she did.

Sam, spotting the woman at the desk, dropped his arm around Beth's shoulders. Leaning close, he whispered in her ear, "I'm not as much of a skeptic any more."

As they approached the desk, the receptionist put the cordless phone back on its stand. At the computer she typed something in and said without looking up at them, "Be with you in a minute."

The buzzer at the door had told her customers had arrived. Only they weren't customers. When Hannah Miller turned toward them, she took one look at Beth and her mouth dropped open. "Beth Crandall? Is that you?"

Beth could hardly contain her excitement as Hannah came out from around the desk and they fell into each other's arms. Tears that had been a long time in coming seeped from her eyes as she and Hannah rocked each other. She had so many questions for Hannah, not the least of which was where had she gotten that black eye she was sporting. Oh, she'd tried to cover it with make-up, but Beth could see the obvious bruising underneath the eye into her cheek.

After they leaned away from each other, Beth said, "I was afraid you wouldn't want to see me. I didn't know where you were transferred to. They wouldn't tell us. And you never contacted me."

"I was sure you'd never want to see me again after what happened. It was *my* fault. I thought your face was terribly damaged. But you hardly have a scar!"

"It wasn't bad. And I had surgery recently to fix it. But we can catch up with that later."

Hannah eyed Sam, and Beth realized she hadn't introduced him.

To Hannah she said, "I brought a close friend with me. Sam Benedict, this is Hannah Miller. Hannah, Sam."

Sam extended his hand to Hannah and she took it hesitantly, shook his briefly, and then pulled away. "So how *did* you find me?" Hannah asked.

Suddenly, however, the door buzzed once more and three men walked in. As they came directly to the desk, Hannah scurried behind it.

Beth said to her, "We'll take a look around." She didn't want to interfere with Hannah's job or get her into trouble.

As Sam wandered a few feet away with her and stopped at a shelf full of fishing gear, he said, "I hope you can have an honest conversation with her."

"Because of the black eye?"

"More than that. She has bruises on her wrists. I saw them when we shook hands. Did you notice how she pulled her sweater sleeve back down again so we wouldn't see?"

"I missed that. I just wanted to soak her in. Her hair's highlighted now though it always did have red lights in it. She was always slender but she seems almost too thin. And she looks tired, like she hasn't been sleeping. Makeup will only cover so much. I'm not exactly sure how to handle it. Do I tell her about Gillian?"

"My guess is you're going to have a lot to catch up on. But I think you should tell her the truth. You both deserve honesty."

That's one of the things she liked about Sam Benedict. The way he saw life and the world—the way he saw her. She'd never had to be anything but honest with him.

After the men at the desk signed up for an evening charter and then left, Beth went to the counter again. "When do you get off work?" Beth asked Hannah.

"Not until seven."

"We can meet for dinner," Sam suggested. "You could come to our hotel. There's a nice restaurant there. Or we could go somewhere you suggest."

Hannah bit her lower lip, obviously trying to decide what was best. "Where are you staying?" she asked.

"At *Seaside View*," Sam responded.

She thought about it some more. "There's a restaurant not far from here that's good called *The Charter*. I can give you the address and directions if you'd like."

"Sam's car has a GPS. If we have the address, we'll be able to find it. What time do you want to meet there?"

"Seven-thirty would be good," Hannah answered as the door buzzed and another customer entered. "We're heading into our busy season. That's why I have to work until seven. Is seven-thirty too late for dinner?"

"It's fine," Beth and Sam said at the same time.

Beth took out one of her business cards with her cell number circled. "That's my cell number. If anything changes, just give me a call. Can I have yours?" She took her phone from her purse and had it ready to add a contact.

Hannah looked uncertain, but then she rattled off a number and Beth added it. "I'm so looking forward to talking to you," Beth said.

"And I'm curious to know how you found me," Hannah returned.

"We'll catch up tonight," Beth promised. She reminded her, "Any change, just give me a call. Sam and I will either be at the hotel or sightseeing."

Hannah checked out Sam again then asked Beth in an undertone, "Boyfriend?"

"Yes," she answered with certainty, thinking about what Sam had said.

"Looks like a good choice," Hannah decided. "But then you can't ever go by looks." She frowned and appeared dejected.

Beth wished customers weren't waiting behind them. "See you soon," she assured Hannah as she and Sam turned and left the office.

Outside, standing in the sunshine, casting their gaze over the boats and the water, Beth determined, "There's something wrong. I don't need Gillian to tell me that."

"We'll find out what it is tonight," Sam said. "Until then, we have time for lunch...and us."

On the drive to Virginia Beach and now again, she had the feeling that something was on Sam's mind. She couldn't do anything about Hannah until they met at seven-thirty so she needed to concentrate on Sam. "Lunch at the hotel?"

"Yes. Then how about if we walk the beach."

For some reason, she had a feeling that a walk on the beach meant a serious conversation. Was she ready for that?

"She's in an abusive situation," Beth said as soon as they were in Sam's car.

"But you don't know what stage of a relationship she's in. Is she still living with her abuser? Has she separated from him? Is she hiding from him?"

"She couldn't be hiding if she's still working at her normal place of employment."

"We can guess all we want, Beth, but we're not going to know until we ask her. And that's my next question to you. Do you want me to come along tonight for dinner? Or do you feel you should talk to her alone?"

"I've gone over a list of pros and cons in my head," she admitted. "But they're about even. One trumps the others. You're wise about relationships. You deal with difficult situations. I think you'd be an asset."

"Now I'm an asset. I'm coming up in the world."

When she glanced at him, she could see a small smile playing on his lips. "You know what I mean. If I get bogged down in something, you can help level it out."

"And if you feel I'm too much of a distraction, or my presence is interfering, I can take a walk."

"If that's okay with you. I wouldn't want you to feel as if I'm tossing you out."

"Beth, there's no right or wrong here. My feelings aren't going to get hurt. They don't get hurt easily."

"Because you deal with insurgents with guns when you're in Africa? I've heard stories. I heard them that night at the gala."

"Those stories tend to be exaggerated. Yes, I've been in some tough situations, and yes, I've had to pick up a gun. But it all turned out. And this...this is not as bad as being invaded by power-hungry rebels, I hope."

"She's into something nasty."

Sam laid his hand on her thigh. "We'll find out what it is and help her if we can. But she has to *want* help, Beth."

Beth thought about that part of the equation as they drove back to their hotel. They ate lunch, talking now and then, gazing into each other's eyes if not at the beautiful ocean view from the windows. The day was balmy, sunny and in the high sixties. They decided not to go back to their rooms, but to go straight to the beach. She'd come prepared. She took a small bottle of suntan lotion from her purse, applied it to her face, then left the purse in Sam's SUV. On the boardwalk, she rolled up her pants legs and spotted the statue of Neptune much farther down the beach. As soon as they were on sand, she slipped off her sneakers and socks, stuffing the socks in the toes.

Sam hadn't worn socks. He rolled up his khakis and slipped off his Docksides. "I wore old ones figuring we'd walk the beach."

"If those are old, I'd like to see new. They don't have a scuff."

"I'm a polish kind of guy…except when I'm not."

She laughed and it felt so good to laugh. Ever since she could remember, she'd felt as if she had a burden resting on her shoulders. As a child, she hadn't really known what it was. As she'd gotten older, she'd realized there was a history behind her life she'd never know. She'd felt she owed it to her adoptive parents to be smiling and grateful and always as happy as she could be…and she'd tried. But there were times when an old sadness weighed her down, times when dark dreams wanted to take over her days too. There were so many times when she just knew she wasn't like everybody else.

Then had come the momentous day when she'd watched that TV interview, had seen Clare, and Max and Amanda and Shara. Since then, she'd felt a different kind of burden—a burden to remember who the Thaddeuses had been as a family, a burden to remember who she'd been as Lynnie Thaddeus.

When she was with Sam, she felt the most normal. She could just be who she was without past burdens and without expectations. He didn't judge her or even expect anything from her. That just boggled her mind.

Now as they began walking the beach, she looked up at him and smiled. "I hope you don't mind that I told Hannah you were my boyfriend."

"We talked about that. I told you that's what I was."

"Just making sure."

He stopped, dropped his shoes, slid his arm around her waist, and brought her close. Without heels she was much shorter than he was. That didn't seem to affect anything now as he bent his head and took a long kiss, right there on the beach.

When he ended it, he said, "No one knows us here, Beth. We can do anything we want."

"On the beach?" she asked with a little laugh.

"Not on *this* beach. But I can imagine a private one somewhere. Or a boat charter where we could go below deck. If that's ever something you want to do, just let me know."

The waves beat on the shore in a primitive, thumping rhythm. Sam's hair blew in the breeze and she realized just how elementally attracted she was to him. "I can't tell if you're teasing or not."

"I'm not teasing," he assured her, his blue eyes as serious as they'd ever been.

After he picked up his shoes and they walked a little farther, he stopped again. "Do you mind getting dirty? I'd like to sit on those boards over there." There was rough hewn driftwood lying on the shore closer to the ocean.

"I don't mind getting sandy. We're at the beach."

Taking her by the hand, he walked with her, then they both sank down onto the driftwood. Staring out at the water for a while, they allowed the peace of the place to settle over them.

Finally Beth said, "You've had something on your mind all day."

"I didn't think you'd see it."

"I've become pretty attuned to you, Sam Benedict. You're quieter than usual."

"Hmmm," he acknowledged. "How did you know I just hadn't had a restless night's sleep?"

"You might have. But that would mean something was on your mind. Spill it."

Taking her hand, he interlaced his fingers with hers. "I told you I'd be flying out of the country again at the beginning of May."

Yes, he had. But she'd been trying to put it out of her mind.

"Well, they'd like me to leave earlier than I'd planned, which would be two weeks from today."

Beth felt as if her heart had stopped for a moment. She only thought of one thing to ask. "How long will you be gone?

"About a month, maybe six weeks."

Six weeks. Right now that seemed like a lifetime long.

Holding her hand on his thigh, he wiggled it. "What are you thinking?"

She sighed. "I'm thinking you're always going to be married to your work." Funny she should use that word married. Just when she'd considered that it could happen to her sometime in the future.

"I love my work, and yes, I have a passion for it. But I also care for you. And I have a suggestion."

She stared at him now. In that moment, she tried to see everything that was in his eyes because she suddenly realized what she was feeling for him was *love*. Did he feel any of that for her?

"We take on volunteers from various organizations who want to do what they consider mission work," he explained. "We give them a basic course in equipment and supplies and what they can and can't do. Of course, they have to have all their vaccinations and a passport. Do you have a passport?"

"I do...for identification purposes. I've never used it."

"Would you like to? Would you like to go with me?"

Beth couldn't have been more shocked by anything he'd asked. "I...don't...know," she confessed haltingly. "Now isn't a good time, not with finding Hannah, with getting to know my family, with Shara having her baby in June—"

"No, the timing isn't ideal, but I suppose it depends on how much you and I mean to each other."

"That's not fair! I recently uprooted my life to move to York for a while. Now you're asking me to uproot it all over again. I'm not the type of person who likes adventure, Sam. You talk about Africa and reference refugee camps and guns."

"Not this trip. It's purely humanitarian."

"You say that, but who knows what can happen overseas. Don't you think I've experienced enough trauma to last a lifetime?"

"Now *you're* not being fair. I do understand what you've been through."

"Do you?" she shot back, wondering if anyone could really understand. She wanted Sam to. "I was a child, kidnapped out of my bedroom in the middle of the night. I was held by a monster who probably did wicked things, so wicked I can't remember anything. We do know now that he murdered two little girls after he let me go. I've always pulled inside myself when I'm scared. I've never felt 'normal.' For all those reasons I built a hard shell around myself. I learned to love my adoptive parents but I didn't let any friends in...until Hannah. I chose web designing for a profession so I could sit in my home and do it all alone. Now you want me to jump into humanitarian work so I can be with you? Yes, I want to be with you. Yes, I want to see where our relationship can go. But not in Africa where I might be afraid of everything I encounter."

Sam stared out at the water rather than looking at her. "My work is my life."

"Why? Why foreign countries? Aren't there enough children here who need your help?"

"There are children here, and I take them on whenever I'm back here. If you could just see the work we do. Would you think about this differently if I were going to Central America?"

"In the middle of all the drug runners?" She shivered.

He frowned, deep lines cutting across his forehead. "So your fears are greater than getting on with your life, with finding a life with me."

"I didn't realize becoming a volunteer to save the world was going to be part of our relationship!" Her voice had risen and she realized just how much she loved Sam and didn't want to see their relationship end.

"I'm not trying to save the world," he protested.

"Then what are you running from?"

He looked startled and snapped, "I'm not running from anything."

"I believe you are. Maybe you're running from your childhood just as I'm running from mine. Are you making this impossible request so we *do* split up? Is that because you're afraid you'd be like your father if you got into a marriage or a serious relationship? You wouldn't, you know. You're a kind, compassionate man. You haven't had a good model for marriage. Maybe that makes you afraid of attempting it."

He cut her a sharp glare. "I didn't say a thing about *marriage.*"

"No, you didn't. Believe me, I understand that. We're just at the boyfriend-girlfriend stage. But now I have to wonder if we'd ever progress beyond that."

He sighed. "We can still be connected if you don't go with me. We can video conference."

"I would suppose your Internet connections will be spotty."

"Maybe. Six weeks isn't a lifetime."

"And what happens when you come back?"

"We can see each other as we are now."

"And then you'll leave again."

He was silent for a while. Finally he admitted, "I don't know what you want me to say or do. I thought I'd found a solution."

The idea of going with him was so big she could hardly wrap her mind around it. "I can't give you an answer now, one way or another. I just can't."

He nodded. "I understand that. But you *will* think about it?"

"Oh, I'll think about it," she assured him, knowing she wouldn't be able to think about much else.

He stood and offered his hand to her. "Let's walk the beach. Maybe the ocean breeze will clear both of our heads."

She would need more than a breeze to clear her head. Yet she took his hand and started walking with him.

Chapter Fifteen

In spite of their argument...or serious discussion...or whatever she wanted to call it, Beth still felt a closeness to Sam. How was that possible when he might fly away and leave her life? But she did. They'd walked and walked and walked along the beach and stared at the ocean. After they'd returned to the hotel, they'd gone to their separate rooms for a while to think about what they'd talked about. After showering and changing for dinner, they met up again in the living room but they hadn't discussed anything serious. Both of them had decisions to make.

With the GPS in Sam's car, they easily found the restaurant where they'd agreed to meet Hannah. They were on time and she wasn't. In fact, fifteen minutes later, after Beth had tried to phone her twice, she wondered if Hannah had decided not to meet them. That would be silly, really, because Beth could simply go back to the place where Hannah worked and ask her what had happened.

But what if something *had* happened?

Sam seemed to be more calm about it than she was. He said, "Let's give her a half hour." At the twenty-five minute mark, Hannah came rushing through the door and began apologizing as soon as she saw them. "I was showing one of the new customers a boat. I lost track of time. And I left my cell phone in my office."

Was she telling the truth?

The hostess came to where they were standing. After determining they needed a table for three, she showed them to one along the windows. Beth and Sam sat side by side across from Hannah. Sam seemed content to let Beth take the lead.

After the waitress brought menus, she said, "We couldn't find a home address for you."

Hannah waved to the menus. "Let's order first, then I'll explain."

Beth noticed that Hannah sounded breezy about it, yet she also noted that Hannah was fidgeting with the edge of the menu. She crossed one leg over the other and her foot was swinging back and forth. Beth knew those signs from when they'd been teenagers. Hannah was agitated and nervous and Beth was determined to find out what about. She didn't want to put Hannah on the defensive but she wanted answers.

After they ordered, she reached across the table and took Hannah's hand. She felt as if their roles were reversed from when they were teens and it felt odd. But something had Hannah spooked, and Beth didn't think it was their appearance into her life. She wasn't exactly sure what to say but everything about her life was straight-forward now. She would have to be that way with Hannah.

"I didn't just hire a private investigator to find you."

"Oh, no? What did you use? A relative in the NSA or something?" Hannah joked, but there seemed to be fear underneath her flip question.

"No, I never thought to go that route. It's a long story as to how I came to know a woman, Gillian Bradley, but she was instrumental in me finding my real family again, the family I was kidnapped from."

"Kidnapped? You were kidnapped? I thought you were abandoned in a mall."

"By my kidnapper. As I said, it's a long story and I can tell you all about it. But for now, I want you to know I found you because I suddenly felt compelled to look for you, as if you needed me."

Hannah's foot stopped swinging under the table. She tried to crack another joke. "You mean like with some woo-hoo connection?"

"If you mean a telepathic connection, maybe it was, maybe it wasn't. Maybe it was karma telling me it was just the right time. But Gillian Bradley has a gift."

Hannah looked confused. "You mean a gift like she's good at numbers? She's good on the computer?"

"No. Some people would call her a psychic."

Hannah's mouth rounded in an O and then she shook her head. "You don't believe in that stuff, do you?"

"She found you. Do you want me to tell you how she did it?"

Hannah looked as if she were ready to jump up and leave. "I don't know if I do. You're kind of freaking me out. I don't know you any more, Beth. Why should I believe anything you're telling me?"

Now Sam stepped in. "First of all, you should believe her because we're here. Whatever we used to find you must have worked pretty well." He kept his tone as placid as Beth had been trying to keep hers.

Hannah looked from one of them to the other and seemed to relax a little. "Where did you drive here from?"

"York, Pennsylvania," Beth responded. "That's where my birth family lives. Years after I was kidnapped, my mom and dad got a divorce. But they reunited when they were looking for their granddaughter who ran away. I have a sister named Clare and it was her daughter Shara who ran off. Gillian helped them find Shara too."

"None of this makes sense," Hannah said, looking again as if she wanted to flee.

"That's because you have to put all the pieces together," Sam reminded her. "Beth was kidnapped when she was three. The man who kidnapped her left her at a mall. She had a lisp and couldn't say her real name. He renamed her and for months he called her Beth, like in *Little Women*. She began to think of herself as Beth. Since she couldn't say her last name which was Thaddeus because of her lisp, she went into the system under the name Beth Saddees. Then the Crandalls adopted her and she became Beth Crandall. But her given name was Lynn Thaddeus."

Silence met Sam's explanation and Beth could see Hannah was trying to absorb the information. Beth said quietly, "I've always been grateful for your protection the night of the attack at the group home. You saved my life."

"You still got cut," Hannah said. "I was so sorry about that."

"It wasn't your fault. Do you remember when Chuck came at me and you stepped between us? I grabbed onto your coat. I inadvertently tore off a button."

"What does that have to do with this?"

"Do you remember?" Beth pressed, knowing if Hannah remembered the details, she could believe what Gillian did much more easily.

Hannah squinted as if trying to make sense of it, as if going back in time. Then she said, "Oh, I remember that coat. It had a big collar and these huge red buttons down the front. After they took you to the hospital, I looked at the coat. It was stupid but I thought it wouldn't close right any more. Nothing would be right any more because somehow I knew I was never going to see you again. I got sent away. The housemom at the new group home sewed a yellow button on the coat and it didn't match at all. I felt freaky. I used red paint in art class one day to paint it. It still didn't match but it was better than the yellow. She'd put a patch on under the button where the material had torn. It looked pretty bad, but it kept me warm." Hannah took a couple of sips from her water glass and then set it back down. "So what about this button?"

"I had it with me at the hospital," Beth explained. "Apparently I had it clutched in my hand and I wouldn't let it go. Mom finally convinced me to give it to her and I did."

"Your adoptive parents were good to you."

"They were...always. I saw a therapist again for a while after the attack," she admitted. "Because night-mares began again."

Hannah's eyes were compassionate when she asked," If you were kidnapped, were you abused?"

"I'm still not sure. Finding my real family again has brought back some memories, and I have to deal with them as they come up, and I will. But I want to talk about you and the red button now."

Hannah murmured, "Okay, talk."

"So my mom kept that button. That night she tucked it into a pocket and forgot about it and ended up taking it home. She put it in her jewelry box and there it stayed until two weeks ago when I told her I wanted to find you. I told her how I was going to find you. She and my dad talked it over and he brought me the button so Gillian could use it."

"Why would this Gillian need the button?"

"I was a skeptic at first," Sam admitted. "But the way they explained it to me was that everything has energy. That button that you fingered when you opened and closed your coat had your energy on it. It even had a small piece of the coat. It hadn't been handled by countless other people, so the energy was still somewhat pure."

Beth took up the story. "So when Gillian held the button, she felt my connection to you. She sensed things about you. *Tide* was one of them. A statue of Neptune was another. Starfish Road was a third. So her partner, who *is* a private investigator, put all the pieces together.

He found an old address listed for you which did him no good. But then he thought about the tide aspect and looked for places of employment that had that in the title. That's how he found *Fit to be Tide*. When he called, acting like a new customer, you answered the phone."

Hannah looked shell-shocked as if she didn't believe any of what she'd just heard. Then she looked Beth straight in the eyes. "You swear this is all true?"

Beth held out her little finger. Hannah curled hers around it and they both said at the same time, "Pinky swear."

"It's a lot to take in," Hannah said. "Especially when I think about the fact that you thought I needed you right now."

"Do you?"

Hannah didn't answer.

Beth wouldn't let her keep silent. She asked softly, "Where did you get the black eye?"

"I should have borrowed actor's make-up instead of buying cheap foundation at the drug store."

"Hannah—" There was a slight scolding note in Beth's voice.

"Look," Hannah said. "I'm in the middle of something and I don't know if I should get you involved. It sounds to me as though you've been through enough."

"We didn't come all this way not to get involved," Sam said.

"I'm not leaving until you tell me the truth," Beth agreed. "Who did that to you?"

"It's funny, really," Hannah said with a humorless chuckle. "I defended you from bullies, but I guess I was placed in one too many foster homes where the 'father' was merely a bully too. The problem was, I wasn't too sure how to handle that kind of bully. I'd had a dad once. I'd listened to him because that was what I was supposed to do. When he left my mom and me, I didn't realize it, but I wanted a replacement. I wanted a mom and I wanted a dad. Every time I was placed in a foster home, I looked for a family. But it was never like that. The mom had her agenda, and the dads certainly had theirs. I tried to please everybody. That was the way to stay out of trouble and to get along. That's the way not to have to go to a new home that could be worse than the one I was in. By the time I was transferred to the group home in Scranton, I didn't think anyone would want me. But I was placed in another foster home. The dad seemed nice at the beginning. He knew how to sweet talk. But as the months went by, he became too familiar. So I ran away, out of the system, out where I could be my own person. I was on the street, in and out of shelters for a year."

"Then you came to Virginia Beach."

"That's right. I'd waitressed and scraped together enough cash in tips for a car and I headed for the beach."

"Why Virginia Beach?" Sam asked.

"I wanted to leave my old life and go someplace warm. I was headed to Florida, hitting several beaches along the way. I couldn't remember which one my mom took me to. But my car broke down and I ended up staying here. I liked it. And the job I found at the marina paid the rent."

Hannah stopped and seemed lost in the past for a few moments. Then she went on, "Jed Wilkins came on as a new employee at the marina eight months ago. He was funny and joked with me and took me on picnics. He was great with a boat, and had his own, just a small one. But still, it was so nice. We got close fast. After a few months, he asked me to move in with him, so I did. I'd never had anybody care about me the way he did. He brought me flowers. On the day I moved in with him, he gave me a necklace that was so pretty."

Beth had a feeling she knew where this was going. "So what happened?" she asked.

"Jed began changing. He still joked but lots of the jokes became cutting at my expense. At first I thought, oh, he just had a bad day. He didn't like the client he took out for the charter. The fish weren't biting— something like that. But when we were with his friends, it got worse. I left one party in tears and went home by myself."

"So you lived with him at his apartment," Sam clarified. "That's why we didn't have an address for you."

"That's right. And he gave me a new phone, too, under his plan. But I started to feel like he wanted control of everything I did. He insisted on knowing every charge that was on my credit card. So I applied for a new one he didn't know about and had the bills sent to a P.O. box. I started to feel even worse than I had when I was in the group home, like I was monitored day and night, had to check in, even had a curfew."

"So what happened?"

"The first time he hit me, we'd been at a party. When we got home, he slapped me. He said I'd said something that embarrassed him in front of his friends and they'd laughed at him. I couldn't even remember what it was. I thought maybe I had. We'd both been drinking. It was possible."

"And the second time?" Beth asked.

"The second time, he had a charter to take out. I was supposed to get home before he was. I got tied up in an accident scene. I was a witness. I didn't have dinner on the table when he got home."

"Where did he hit you that time?" Sam asked.

"He wrenched my arm and bruised my shoulder by throwing me against a door. I rationalized. I said he hadn't hit me. He'd just pushed me. But I thought about leaving, and I packed an emergency bag."

"And then?" Beth prompted.

"He found out about the P.O. box. I don't know if he was following me or had a friend follow me or what. I just know I got home from work and there he was. He grabbed me by the wrists, shook me so hard my teeth rattled. Then he socked me and gave me the black eye. He tried to punch my stomach but I was too fast. I pushed him over, managed to grab my bag that I'd hidden under my bed, and told him I was going to the police. That stopped him. He begged me, started crying, saying he'd never do it again. But I didn't believe it. So I jumped in my car and drove to the police station. They helped me find a lawyer to get a restraining order—an order of protection. So now I'm staying with a friend and just letting things cool down. I like my job and I don't really want to leave it. They fired Jed so I don't have to worry about him being around my work place."

Sam couldn't keep his opinion to himself. "I don't like this, Hannah. He has several reasons to want revenge on you."

"But I'm with people at work, and I'm with a friend at night. He doesn't know who I'm staying with."

Sam gave Beth a look, then said to Hannah, "You think he's moved on?"

"I haven't heard from him for a week. Everything's quiet. There's been no sign of him. I'm hoping he *has* moved on. Maybe when we're finished dinner, you can come back to Leah's place with me. You can see I'm fine. The black eye's healing now, and soon I'll be looking for an apartment on my own again. I'm going to be okay, Beth."

How Beth wanted to believe that. But whether it was her heart or intuition, she didn't believe it. She turned to Sam. "Is it okay if we go back to her friend's place? I'd like to meet her."

"Sure, it's fine. We're staying over tonight. We don't have to leave early in the morning. I'm always ready to meet new people," he said with a shrug.

The three of them enjoyed dinner after that. Hannah and Beth caught up, and Sam explained about his practice. Beth told Hannah about Max and Amanda's wedding, Clare and Joe, and how Shara was going to keep her baby.

Hannah said, a bit enviously Beth thought, "So now you have two families?"

"I do, and I'm just trying to figure out how we all fit together."

Suddenly Hannah's phone buzzed from her purse. She glanced toward it.

Beth said, "Go ahead."

"I'll just check and see who it is. Jed stopped leaving messages."

She took her phone out and checked the screen. Her brow crinkled. "It's Leah, the friend I'm staying with. I told her I was having dinner with a friend so I don't know why she's calling. I'd better take it."

Across the table from Hannah, Beth and Sam could hear every word because her friend's voice was loud.

"You got a huge bouquet of flowers from Jed," her friend said, sounding panicked.

"That's not possible. How would he know I'm staying with you?"

"Maybe because you don't have that many friends and I'm one of them. You can't stay here, Hannah, not if he's going to come after you. He could have a weapon...or anything. Come get your things. You have to go somewhere else."

"I don't have anywhere else to go."

"Call your boss."

"I can't do that. Myron has two little girls. I'm not going to take the chance that Jed would show up there."

Sam leaned toward Beth and whispered in her ear. "We'll take her with us."

Beth took hold of his arm. Did he really want to get mixed up in this? "Are you sure?"

He nodded.

Beth reached across to Hannah to get her attention. "Tell your friend you're going to stop by to pick up your things. We'll take you to our hotel."

Hannah looked totally scared. "But if he sent the

flowers, he might be watching for me there. If he sees me pick up my things—"

Sam's deeply gentle voice was reassuring as he said, "Believe me. I'll make sure no one follows us."

To reinforce Sam's statement, Beth added, "Sam's had to deal with renegades in refugee camps. He knows what he's doing."

Hannah's eyes were still wide and frightened, but she put her phone back to her ear. "I'll be there in ten to pick up my things. Then you won't have to worry any more." She ended the call, obviously deflated by her friend's lack of loyalty, by her friend's fear for her own safety, no matter what Hannah was going to face.

Hannah studied first Beth and then Sam. "I don't know what he'll do next. Are you sure about this?"

Sam gave Beth a signal to slide out of the booth. "You two go to the car. I'll pay the bill. We'll get this done and get you safe."

After Beth and Hannah went to the car, Beth used the remote and opened it with the keys that Sam had given her. They slid in and shut the doors.

"What am I going to do, Beth? I can't stay at your hotel with you. I mean, not past a night or maybe two. I have to work but he'll follow me there."

Sam opened the driver's side door then and slid in. "Tell me where to go. Beth can stay in the car and keep watch. I'll go in with you to pick up your things. She can text me or call me if she sees anything iffy." Sam reached over and put his hand on Beth's shoulder. "Are you okay with that? It seems to be the safest. No one will even know you're in the car."

She could see his point. She'd rather go in with Hannah but it was safer this way. "I'll make sure no one follows you inside. If I see anybody hanging around, or even a car that looks suspicious, I'll call you."

Sam nodded and switched on the ignition.

Hannah's friend only lived about a mile away. Sam drove slightly above the speed limit, and they arrived there minutes later. In the darkness Beth didn't know what she was going to be able to see, but she'd keep watch of all the lighted areas and the shadowed areas around those.

They parked in one large lot that spanned the course of three buildings. Hannah said, "I'm staying on the second floor in the middle building."

"Is there a back entrance?" Sam asked.

"Not for the public. There's a fire door."

"That sounds more complicated than just going in quickly and getting your things. Come on." Sam leaned over and gave Beth a quick kiss. "This won't take long," he said.

Beth hoped it wouldn't because she'd be a nervous wreck the whole time they were inside.

"I'm going to leave the keys," Sam told her. "Just in case you need them for some reason."

She wasn't sure what that meant, but she'd never driven an SUV this big. If she had to...well, she guessed she'd have to.

"Stay down," Sam told her. "I don't want anyone to see you when I open the door."

Were these precautions really necessary? she wondered. But then she realized Sam knew about the mind of an abuser first-hand. Holding onto the keys Sam had given her, she ducked down. But as soon as the front and the back doors were closed again, she popped back up. Sam had parked in an area of the lot where no lights shone on the car. He really did know what he was doing.

She tried not to tick off the minutes in her mind while she waited. She imagined Hannah looking at the flowers, going to her room, throwing things into a suitcase or a duffel bag. How much had she taken along to her friend's? Sam was probably convincing her to just take the essentials, to either leave the rest or have it sent to her once she was someplace safe. Beth realized that even after only knowing Sam as long as she had, she understood how he thought, how he planned, how he cared.

All at once Beth was aware of what sounded like a truck idling somewhere nearby. As she took note of the cars parked in the parking lot, she caught sight of the outline of a truck on the north side of the lot. Maybe someone was leaving. The thing was, she hadn't noticed anyone come out of any of the three buildings. That truck had just started up as if it had been waiting for someone. She took a deep breath, getting a funny feeling up her spine. The hairs at the nape of her neck prickled. Everything about this situation was screaming danger. Call Sam? Yes. She had to listen to her gut.

Keeping her phone way down near the seat so the glow couldn't be seen outside the windows, she texted him. **Possible stalker in the parking lot. What should I do?**

He texted right back. **Give me a minute.**

The truck's engine still idled.

Not long after, another text came through from him. **Can you crawl over the console into the driver's seat?**

She looked at the console and knew she could clamber over it. She texted back, **Yes.**

There's a driveway next to building C. It will take you around back. It's only wide enough for one car, he texted.

She realized Hannah or Leah must be feeding him this information.

The text continued, **Count to 25 then drive around back. We'll be at the door and climb right into the SUV.**

You expect me to lose him? she texted, scared now.

We'll do it together. You can do this, Beth. We'll head down the fire stairway. Count to 25.

What Sam didn't know was that she was shaking. The whole idea of this made her feel sick in the stomach and a little bit woozy. It wasn't the first time she'd felt it. Somewhere in the deepest recesses of her mind, she remembered a dark night, a shadowed figure scooping her up from her bed. She remembered a calloused hand clamped over her mouth. A beard. A sweaty male scent. She remembered—

Taking a huge breath, she remembered what she was supposed to do. Keys in hand, she somehow managed to crawl over the console into the driver's seat. She didn't fasten her seat belt because she didn't know what was going to happen next. But she started counting. She made herself think one-thousand one, one-thousand two, one-thousand three, so that she wouldn't rush. After one-thousand twenty-five, she took another deep breath, put the key in the ignition, and turned it. The vehicle roared to life and she took off, knowing surprise was their best defense.

The buildings themselves were lit up fairly well. She could easily see where she was driving. She could see the buildings outlined with track lighting along each floor on the outside of the apartments. Even though she knew she was coming up on the fire door at the middle building, she didn't know exactly where it was.

She skidded to a stop. As she did, she saw headlights appear in her rearview mirror. Were Sam and Hannah there? Were they ready?

Her heart seemed to stop when she thought they weren't. But then suddenly they burst through the door. Sam and Hannah both scrambled into the back seat.

The pickup truck was coming closer. Beth hardly waited till that back door was shut again and she zoomed away.

Sam had his hand on her shoulder. "Good job. I'll watch him. You just drive. Make either a left turn or a right turn as soon as you can. If you see a driveway between buildings, take it."

"I don't know if I can do this," she muttered.

"Yes, you can. You know you can. *I* know you can."

His confidence spurred her on, especially when he said, "It's not speed that matters. It's strategy and the turns you make. If you can run a yellow light, do it. He'll get caught by red."

She made several sharp turns, as sharp as they could be in an SUV. Still those headlights followed which proved just one thing to her. This Jed Wilkins was determined. He wanted Hannah and he was going to get her.

"I could call the police," Hannah said.

"It's too dark to see to know for sure it's him. The license plate is muddy and I can't read it. No proof, Hannah."

"He's going to have to hurt me for them to do something, isn't he?"

"Not if we can help it," Beth assured her. She suddenly saw an alley. She didn't know where it went. If it was a dead end, they were out of luck. They could end up facing off with whoever was in that truck. Of course, then they *could* call the police.

She took the alley with a squeal of tires. It wasn't a dead end, thank goodness. She took a fast left out of it, spun onto a more heavily trafficked road, and changed lanes.

"Good move," Sam congratulated her. "Now if you can just make it through that yellow light."

She did.

Sam kept watch and so did Hannah. As she merged with more traffic, it was harder to tell if they were being followed. But they were nearing the area where their hotel was located.

Sam suggested, "Turn down a side street. Let's see if we lost him."

Beth turned down more than one side street, but no one followed them.

"I'll drive to our hotel," she said. "Once we're inside, security will be on our side."

Letting her heart settle into a more normal rhythm, she added, "I hate to bring this up, but what if he goes to Leah to find out where you've gone?"

"We didn't tell her where we were going," Sam said. "And Leah's boyfriend was there. Guys like this are usually bullies with women, not with other men. I told her to call 9-1-1 if he shows up."

"Won't the police think I'm crazy doing this over a bouquet of flowers?" Hannah asked.

"No. He broke the restraining order. My guess is that it specified *no contact*."

"It did. But I wasn't there."

"You need to stay far away from him, Hannah," Sam advised her.

"But how am I going to do that if I'm in Virginia Beach?"

Beth felt a calm come over her, and she knew how to answer that question. "You're not going to stay in Virginia Beach. You're going to come back to York and stay with me."

Chapter Sixteen

Max liked his new life. He appreciated his renewed marriage. He gave thanks every day that Beth had come home. Yes, he wanted to call her Lynnie, but that wasn't who she was now. After she'd been kidnapped, after he'd searched and searched and searched, hounded the police, fallen into the deep depths of Jack Daniels, he'd known what despair was. During that terrible time, he and Amanda had grown farther and farther apart, and somehow in the whole mess, he'd ignored the daughter who'd remained.

Now, however, life had taken a decided upturn. He felt like part of his family again. He and Amanda had connected the way they had when they'd first met on her dad's farm. Old was new. Amazing!

As he watched his wife get ready for bed, he felt so blessed. It was an odd word for him to use when for years he'd railed at God and lost his faith. Did he have it back? He was getting there. He was getting there because of the women in his life—Amanda, Clare,

Shara, Beth, and even Gillian Bradley. She'd given him back hope.

Amanda stood at the dresser brushing her strawberry-blond hair and he realized she was more attractive to him than she'd ever been. She was wearing a flowered silky nightgown and he couldn't wait until she was lying beside him.

Continuing to brush her hair, she asked, "What do you think will come of Beth's search for Hannah?"

"I'm hoping she's not kicking a hornet's nest." Finding a best friend was one thing. Releasing a nasty nest of memories was another.

Amanda's thoughts must have been running similar to his. She turned to face him. "Because of the memories she could let loose?"

"Yes. If anything could bring them back, I would imagine this would."

"You didn't say whether you think it's a good idea that Sam went with her."

"I didn't say because I don't know. I did ask him to watch over her."

"Does she know that?"

"That depends on whether or not he tells her. But those two seem to be pretty honest with each other."

"Too honest?" Amanda asked with raised brows.

"I didn't say that. At the place where Beth is in her life I'm not sure she can be too honest. The question is whether Sam's ready to hear her honesty or not."

"I don't understand," Amanda said, setting down her brush.

"Even *I* could see the connection between them when

we had dinner. Is that good for Beth? Maybe. Is it good for Sam? That depends. He has concentrated on nothing but his work for years. Can he make room for someone as exceptional as Beth?"

"Do you mean as needy?"

"She needs a man's understanding and compassion and full attention. I don't know if Sam can give her that."

"Have you talked to her about this?"

"No, because if she's anything like Clare, she'll rebel against whatever I say."

"She's not like Clare," Amanda insisted. "You know that."

"No, but she also still doesn't think of herself as my daughter, which means there would be a barrier to begin with. I'd be like a stranger giving advice."

Amanda went over to the bed and sat on his side next to his hip. "Does that hurt you?"

"If it does, I ignore it. I'm just so happy she's back. I'm just so happy that Luther Brown didn't kill her spirit."

"I still think of her as Lynnie," Amanda said in a soft voice.

"I know you do, but she'll never be Lynnie Thaddeus again."

"If she and Sam really get involved, maybe she'll stay in York."

"He's leaving for Africa again in May. She might go back to Pittsburgh while he's not here. And if you decide to sell the business, she won't have a place to live."

"She'll always have a place to live. She can stay with us."

He brushed his wife's hair away from her cheek. "You know she wants to be independent. Look how she decided to pay part of her surgery charges. She needs her own place."

Amanda was quiet for a few seconds then admitted, "I've been thinking more about hiring someone to manage the business end of *Yesteryear's Treasures*. I would still be the main buyer. I could do much of it online. I'd consult constantly with a manager, of course. But a store manager would be there day to day to deal with the customers, to handle the bookwork program, to take the load off of me. Clare could work and I could be Shara's babysitter. She can go to school, and I'll care for the baby."

"Would that be best for Shara?" Max wondered.

"She wouldn't have to take a full course load at first. Maybe she could even take some of the classes online. But I could be there to help out any way she needed me."

"Are you willing to let go of *Yesteryear's Treasures?*"

"Not completely. But that way Beth would still have the apartment above the store whenever she wanted it."

"You're not trying to fix everything, are you?" he asked in a teasing tone.

"I know better than to think I can fix *anything*. Just look at Clare and Joe. Do you think what Joe's proposing could possibly work? Do you think Clare will take the leap of selling her house? I'm not giving any advice on that front."

Max laughed. "Come here," he said, sliding to the middle of the bed to make room for her on his side.

"I didn't put lotion on my face yet."

He ran his finger down her cheek. "You don't need lotion on your face."

After a moment's hesitation, she agreed. "Maybe not tonight I don't." She slipped in beside him, fitting next to him as if her body was made to be spooned next to his.

Hannah's hands were still shaking as Beth sat beside her on the sofa in the living room of her hotel suite. Sam had gone to his bedroom to give them privacy.

"Are you sure you want me to come home with you?" Hannah asked for at least the fifth time.

"I'm positive. It's the only safe thing for you to do. You have to get away from here, and you have to go somewhere where he can't find you. As far as Jed knows, you have no connection to anyone in Pennsylvania."

"Before we leave tomorrow, I'll empty my bank account so I can take that along. Thank goodness I have money saved. Sometimes I go along on bigger charter boats and act as a sort of waitress. I get tips. For the most part, I socked them away."

"When we get to York, we'll talk to Max, my birth dad. He's a lawyer. He can help figure out the best way to keep you safe."

"I can't believe you came into my life right now. What kind of coincidence is that?"

Beth shook her head. "I don't think it *is* a coincidence. I can't explain it, but I think it's more than fate."

"All things work together..." Hannah quoted part of the Bible verse.

"Something like that. But it's about connections too. Maybe some deep part of me just knew you were in trouble, just like Gillian can find missing persons."

"When we get to York, I'm going to have to get a job as soon as I can. I don't want to deplete the money I have."

"Maybe Max will have ideas about that."

"If I use my Social Security number and credit cards, Jed will eventually be able to find me."

"Do you think he'd go to those lengths? Is he smart enough to do it himself?"

"No. I don't think he is. But he has computer geek friends. They might be."

"Again, that's something we'll talk to Max about—whether or not you should register your order of protection in Pennsylvania. If you do, it will be a matter of public record. Max also has good contacts at the police department. He'll know how to best keep you safe."

"I've been so afraid ever since this…" She touched the remnants of bruises around her eye. "Ever since the last time he hit me. I even thought about buying a gun."

"I thought about that when I rented my first apartment," Beth admitted. "Of course, no one was coming after me then but shadows of the past. I decided *not* to buy a gun because I just didn't want to have it around. I did buy a can of wasp spray."

"Wasp spray," Hannah said with a little laugh. "I never thought of that. I suppose that could be as damaging as mace."

"Think about it. If you buy a gun, you need to go to the training that's necessary with it. It's the only safe thing to do."

Hannah nodded.

After Beth stood, she took a seat cushion from the sofa. "Let's pull this open so you can get a good night's sleep. If I know Sam, he'll want to eat breakfast and be at the bank as soon as it opens so we can be on our way."

"Do you *really* know Sam?"

Beth realized what Hannah was asking. Did she know Sam well enough to give him her heart? Did she know him well enough to consider what he wanted her to do—go to a foreign country with him? Did she know him well enough to make love with him?

"I've known him since January when I consulted with him about my scar. But I feel as if I've known him so much longer. Maybe because I feel as if I don't just know his mind, but his heart too."

"I was blinded by pretty words and charm," Hannah confessed. "I never realized I was being manipulated. You and Sam seem to have something really honest."

After a hug, Beth left Hannah on the sofa with a mug of herbal tea on the coffee table and everything she needed to think about. Beth went to her own room to change before saying good-night to Sam. But in her own room she thought about how she wanted to say good-night, *if* she wanted to say good-night...or if she wanted more. She found herself showering, taking extra care when she blew her hair dry. She'd brought along a simple yellow nightgown with a pink and yellow flowered robe. She put them on, her stomach feeling a little upside-down excited. From the adrenaline rush of their escapade tonight?

No. From the pictures forming in her mind...and heart. Common sense, though, prevailed and she developed a plan. She was just going to say good-night to him and see where it led. If Sam was leaving the country and she didn't go with him, they wouldn't have much time left together. She was learning to make the most of every minute, to follow her instincts as she never had before.

Tonight her instincts led her barefooted to Sam's door at the end of the hall. He'd left his door slightly ajar.

She rapped lightly and peeked inside. He was sitting at the table with a laptop in front of him. He'd changed into a T-shirt and running shorts. She swallowed hard. Maybe this wasn't such a good idea after all.

He looked over at her, his expression concerned. "Is Hannah settled in?"

"Yes, she is. I just wanted to come and say good-night, but I don't want to bother you if you're working."

Standing, he crossed to her. "Just catching up with the office. I e-mailed them that I'd be back tomorrow and could do rounds on Friday."

"Hannah would like to stop at the bank before we leave tomorrow."

"That's fine. We can do that on the way out. No one followed us here so we shouldn't have any problems."

"She's asking all kinds of questions that I don't have the answers to. I'm hoping Max can help."

"If necessary, she can change her name legally."

"But won't that take time to do?"

"Max could probably expedite it. He probably has favors he can call in. We'll talk to him when we get back."

They stared at each other for long moments. She cleared her throat and said, "I don't know what I would have done without you on this trip. If I'd come down here by myself, there might have been a different outcome."

"You're smart. You and Hannah would have figured something out." He was looking at her as if he'd never seen a woman in her nightgown and robe before.

She felt self-conscious. "I guess I shouldn't have come in here like this."

A half smile played across his lips. "That depends. If I close that door, we can explore each other in a way we haven't before. But are you ready for that?"

Still a little unsure, she countered with, "If you kiss me, we'll find out just how ready I am."

Sam bent his head and did just that. Then he closed the door.

When Beth awakened in the middle of the night, Sam's arms were wrapped around her and she'd never felt safer. Sam had been a wonderfully considerate and gentle lover yet they'd both experienced pleasure that had left them breathless. She'd been prepared for feelings of panic, the fact that they might have to stop what they were doing if a flashback suddenly washed over her. But that hadn't happened! It was a miracle, really.

She began to wonder now if Luther Brown *had* done the things to her that an adult should never do to a child. She began to wonder if, instead, he'd kidnapped her and kept her simply to dress her up and name her and treat her like a doll before his pedophile propensities had escalated. If that had been the case, she was *more* than lucky. If that had been the case, she'd been blessed. In a way, coming back to her family and this search for Hannah was resolving all the questions from her past. It had been such a murky past and it still was in many respects. But she was finding answers in her thoughts, in her feelings, and especially in being with Sam. Always before, fear had kept her from dating and kept her from looking at a man twice...had kept her running if one had looked at her.

But Sam...he seemed to be exactly what she needed...*who* she needed. When she was with him, her past and the present seemed to come together and weren't as confusing.

Still the question remained—could she follow him across continents and be part of his work? Did she want that, even though she wanted *him*?

She'd have to find the answer to that question and find it soon. But for now, she burrowed her face against his chest, breathed in his scent, and held on tight.

Awakening with a woman in his arms was an odd experience for Sam. Light from a new day spilled in the windows around the draperies. He suddenly realized he'd held Beth throughout the night. He wanted to keep holding her now.

In all his romantic past, if he could call it that, he'd never slept with a woman through the night and awakened with her in the morning. In med school he hadn't had time for relationships what with his studies, an internship, his residency, a fellowship. All of it had kept him single-minded in purpose and focused on his life's work. When he had taken time for physical pleasure with a woman, they'd both known the score. He wouldn't be committing to anything. He had places to go, children to fix, work that was more important than any affair of the heart.

He looked down at Beth now and felt such protective tenderness, his heart actually hurt. His throat became tight. He felt unsettled and troubled and all together confused.

He was committed to the work he did, wasn't he? Africa had been in the works for months. There was always some place he needed to be.

Yet Beth's questions from their discussion on the beach haunted him. Was he running *away* from something rather than *toward* something? Why couldn't he stay in the United States and just help children here? Did he need the acclaim for doing good work? Had glad-handing donors and dealing with red tape become part of his existence because he wanted to do it? All of the busyness and buzz and PR, as well as the traveling, could be keeping him from a real life.

Just *what* did he want?

If Beth accompanied him on this Africa trip, would that cement their relationship or tear them apart? Would she see who he really was? A doctor who cared about children, yes, but a man who had never really faced his background and what it meant to his future, afraid he'd be like his father?

That was a dark virus that maybe had shaded everything he did. Maybe he *was* running so he didn't have to find out.

Holding Beth a little tighter, he knew he had to eradicate that virus or he could never be happy.

When they reached York early the following evening, Beth realized they were all tired from wrapping up Hannah's life in Virginia Beach. On the drive back, Beth had phoned Gillian and filled her in on everything that had happened. Afterward, Sam had insisted they stop at a restaurant to eat and stretch. That had been the doctor talking. Hannah had been supremely quiet during the road trip—probably thinking about her future.

After Sam helped Hannah and Beth bring their bags up to the apartment above *Yesteryear's Treasures*, he said, "I'm going to stop in at my office. Do you two want to have dinner alone, or should I stop and get take out and bring it back here?"

Beth and Hannah exchanged a look and then Hannah nodded. Beth knew what that meant— Hannah didn't mind Sam's company, and she knew Beth wanted to be with him.

"I probably only have the makings for omelets in the fridge. Take out would be great. But can you make sure we have enough for four? I'm going to call Clare. I want her to meet Hannah."

"How about Amanda?" he asked.

"I'll call her too and see if we can't set up something to meet with her and Max tomorrow. That way Hannah can find out what she needs to do to keep safe."

"Sounds like a plan. I'll bring an assortment of Chinese and enough just in case Amanda decides to stop by too."

"You're right. She might. With or without Dad."

Sam's brows arched, and Beth suddenly realized what she'd said. "If I start calling Max *Dad*, it's going to be confusing. I'll have Dad number one and Dad number two, and I don't want either to get insulted."

"Do you think Max might go for the name Pops?"

Beth had to laugh. "He might. I'll try it on him next time I see him." She pointed to the bedrooms. "Hannah, your bedroom is the one in the back. It's small with a single bed."

"It will be fine," Hannah assured her. "I'd be glad just for your couch."

"There aren't any closets in that room. The door in the back opens to a stairway that leads downstairs to a storeroom. But I have room in my closet so you can hang clothes in there."

"I don't have much to worry about right now. Tomorrow maybe you can point me in the direction of a discount store. After Myron sells my car for me, he'll send me a cashier's check and I can tuck that money away too."

Early this morning, Hannah had phoned her boss to tell him what was happening. They'd dropped off her car keys and the title to the car before they'd left. Her quick visit there had given her the chance to thank him and say good-bye. Sam had taken circuitous routes to and from and no one had followed them.

Now Hannah pulled out the handle on her roller bag. "I'll start unpacking." She gave Beth a wink then went down a short hall to her bedroom.

Sam smiled down at Beth. "I think she knows I want to kiss you before I leave."

Beth wrapped her arm around his waist as they walked into the kitchen to the door.

After Sam opened the door, they stood there simply gazing at each other. "We haven't been alone enough today to talk about last night and where we go from here," he said.

"I want to spend more nights like that with you," she told him.

Wrapping his arms around her, he assured her, "And I want more nights like that with you. Maybe afternoons, too."

She laughed. She was still smiling when his lips covered hers.

After he ended the kiss, he blew out a breath. "I'm definitely going to have to sneak you away from Hannah for alone time. With the weekend, that should be easier to do."

"If I'm with you, I want to make sure Hannah's with someone else—Clare or Amanda. I'll feel better knowing she has support and is safe."

"I'll help you do that. I know there's a support group that meets in our office complex. Do you think she'd go? She needs at least the group counseling so she doesn't get into another relationship like that."

"I'll talk to her about it," Beth said.

"She really got off easy, Beth. I've had to repair the damage done by abusive husbands or boyfriends. But she's got to get her head in the right place so she doesn't start another relationship like that."

"How can you tell if a relationship will be abusive?"

"There are signs. Maybe not right at the beginning because some of these guys can be really charming. But eventually the control issues come up. Hannah didn't have any relatives or many friends to cut her off from. But he would have tried to do that too. She might need to register that protective order in Pennsylvania. The two of you can talk to Max about that tomorrow."

"Will you be gone long?" she asked.

"Probably about an hour. I have papers to sign at the office and charts to look at. What's your favorite Chinese entrée?"

"Sweet and Sour Chicken," she said without hesitation.

"I'll make sure I pick up one of those." He gave her a hug and another quick kiss. His hands lingered on her arms as if he didn't want to let her go. But then he did.

She stared after him as he jogged down the steps, wondering again where they were going to go from here.

Chapter Seventeen

While Hannah unpacked, Beth called Clare and filled her in on what had happened. Her sister said, "Smart moves on your part and Sam's." Clare was met with silence and seemed to be waiting for a response.

Finally, Beth said, "Sam's terrific in a crisis situation."

"And how about when it's not a crisis situation?"

Beth lowered her voice because if there was one person she could tell this to, it was her sister. "We made love, and it was wonderful."

"Wow! I didn't expect that," Clare responded. "Did you handle everything okay?"

"I did. And it makes me think that, well, maybe Luther Brown didn't touch me, not in that way."

"Oh, Beth, I'm so happy for you! I want to hear all about it."

"I don't know if I want to tell you all about it," she said smiling. "It's between me and Sam. You don't want to talk about your love life with Joe, do you?"

"At least I can say I have one again," Clare said honestly. "We're working things out. I'm going to sell my house, and Shara and I are going to move in with him...into his dad's place. His dad's going to buy a condo. We're making a few renovations to his dad's house and I don't know how fast this is going to happen. We'd like to get it all done before the baby's born."

"I'll help you any way I can, but..." She hesitated. "Sam has asked me to go with him on his trip to Africa."

"You're kidding."

"No. I don't know if I want to. But if I don't, I don't know what will happen between us. It's all so confusing right now, and with Hannah thrown in...I'm just not really sure about anything except that I do love Sam."

"Hold on a minute, I want to ask Joe something."

It wasn't long until Clare was back on the line. "I'm going to come over and meet Hannah. Joe said he'll stay here with Shara. Maybe the three of us can delve into the psyche of men."

"Okay. That sounds good. I'm going to give Amanda a call. I want to set up a meeting with Max for tomorrow with Hannah. She needs legal advice."

"I'll say. I'll see you in about a half hour."

Beth went into the bedroom and saw that Hannah was making herself at home. "I'm sorry there's only one bathroom. We'll have to share."

"No problem there. You're lucky to have a place this nice."

"Mom...I mean Amanda...lived here after she got her business started. She furnished it with many of the antiques she bought for the store. She changes out the furniture now and then. I haven't bothered to really make it my own place because I don't know how long I'm staying."

"It's tough to be torn between two families."

That was exactly the way Beth felt—torn. "If you're okay, I'm going to call Amanda and set up something to meet with her and Max tomorrow."

"I'm good. I'll get a shower while you're doing that."

As Beth returned to the living room, she realized how the word "Mom" had slipped out again. When she thought of Amanda, she could imagine a younger version of her for just a flash. She imagined her holding a hose in the backyard of a house. Beth and Clare were running through it, having a grand old time. Was it an actual memory? She hadn't looked through photograph albums that Amanda had kept because she didn't want to be confused if memories did come back. She didn't want to confuse a memory with seeing a picture in an album. She'd have to ask Clare about the backyard and the hose.

Her conversation with Amanda didn't go as smoothly as her conversation with Clare had gone. She'd been tempted to downplay exactly what had happened yet she couldn't because she needed Max's help and maybe Amanda's too. So she told her everything.

Amanda was horrified. "You could have been hurt, if not by that terrible man, then by a car accident with trying to outrun him. What was Sam thinking?"

"Mom, we all did the best we knew how."

The sudden silence made Beth realize what she'd said.

In a shaky voice, Amanda said, "You called me *Mom*."

Now what to say? Or do? "I have a lot to tell you and some decisions to make. But the search for Hannah has brought back some good memories of you and Max. And now and then I find myself thinking in terms of you and Max as Mom and Dad."

"Oh, Lynnie."

"I'm never going to be Lynnie again, you know," Beth reminded Amanda.

"I know. You've grown into Beth Lynn Crandall, but I still think of you as my Lynnie. I try not to let it slip out, but sometimes it just does, when I'm talking to your dad or to Clare."

"I don't mind," Beth said, meaning it. After they both took a little pause, Beth asked, "Do you know Max's schedule for tomorrow? I'd like to bring Hannah to meet the two of you, and she needs his advice, legal advice. Do you think he can help with that?"

"I'm sure he can. He had a meeting tonight at the Youth Center, but as soon as he gets home I'll have him give you a call. And Beth, these decisions you have to make, do they have to do with Sam?"

"They do, and I need to know something, something a mom would tell her daughter."

"What, honey?"

"Why did you and Max get back together again after so many years apart? How could you forget about the trauma and the divorce and what separated you?"

After a few moments of consideration, her mother revealed, "I think it all boiled down to the fact that we'd never stopped loving each other, even though we hurt each other. I go to AA meetings with your dad now and then. He's so honest about what he thinks and feels now. We talk about the years in between. We both changed with being alone...with having different life responsibilities. But one thing had never changed. When we got married we made a promise. Life got in the way. But that promise was like a cord that could never be severed. Finally we realized we still believed in that promise and we renewed it again."

"Thank you for telling me."

"Some day I hope you'll make the wedding promise that will last a lifetime. I love you, Beth."

"I love you too...Mom."

Beth could hear the catch in her mother's voice when she said, "I'll have your dad call you as soon as he gets in."

Beth held the phone for a moment and thought about the conversations she'd just had with Clare and with her mother, her birth mother. She hoped she could explain to her adoptive mom how and why all of it had come about. But she'd save that for later.

Beth decided she'd change and freshen up. After all, this would be a kind of date with Sam tonight even if a lot of people were around. She slipped into a pair of dark purple leggings and pulled out a sky-blue and lilac tunic that Clare had insisted she buy. It had a wide cowl neck, long slim sleeves and a tulip-cut hem. She'd never given much thought to stylish clothes before, but now she wanted to. At her neck she hung a necklace on a gold chain. The pendant was a circle with a small diamond set in the center. Her parents, her adoptive parents, had given it to her on her twenty-first birthday. She liked it and often wore it for a special occasion. In a way, this was a very special occasion.

Would Clare and Hannah like each other?

Their first visit could very well set the tone for their future.

Hannah stopped in the doorway to Beth's room. She'd redone her makeup until the bruises almost didn't show at all. Her face looked more relaxed without the worry creases on her brow. She was wearing blue jeans and a geometrically printed long-sleeved crop top.

"Do you want me to get out dishes…set the table… anything?"

"My table really only seats two comfortably, so we'll probably eat in the living room. I think I remember some folding TV tables that are downstairs in the storage room. They haven't been entered into the inventory yet. Why don't you get plates and put them on the coffee table. I'll go get the tables."

As Hannah went to the kitchen, Beth hurried through Hannah's bedroom to the door that led downstairs. She ran down the stairs to the storage room and looked for the tables. She had a terrible time finding them. Amanda's assistant must have moved them. Abandoning the storage room, she went into the back of the shop and there they were, leaning against the counter. It seemed odd that Amanda would consider not coming back to the shop…that she'd consider selling the business. She must really be embracing the idea of becoming a great grand-mother. It would be another huge shift in perspective.

The tables weren't that heavy but they were bulky. As Beth carried the set up the stairs, she heard noise up above. Something shattered. Had Hannah dropped a plate? A glass? Beth hurried her pace. At the top of the stairs she set the tables down with a sigh of relief. They'd gotten heavier than she'd expected.

There was a low rumble of voices—one a male voice—and Beth wondered if Sam had returned with take-out. She picked up the tables again and exited the guest bedroom into the hall. As she did, she recognized Hannah's voice but not the man's.

Suddenly Hannah yelled, "No! No! I'm not going. Let go of me."

Let go of me. Let go of me. The words echoed in Beth's head. One of those vague memories, her kicking her legs. She was trying to tell that tall bearded man she didn't want to go with him. Then he put something over her nose and her mouth, something that smelled funny. *Let go. Let go.* The words haunted her again. Another image—her trying to pull away from the man. But she couldn't and he pushed her into a room and then locked the door. She sank down on the floor and cried and cried and cried. She missed her mommy. She missed her daddy. She missed her sister.

Hannah's voice coming from the kitchen brought her back to the present. "I'm *never* going back to Virginia with you. Not ever. You hurt me."

In that moment of clear insight, Beth realized Hannah's ex-boyfriend had found her...had found *them*. But he didn't know Beth was here, did he?

Carefully, so the floors wouldn't creak, Beth stepped into her bedroom and set down the tables. Slipping off her shoes so she didn't make any noise, she went to her nightstand. The can of wasp spray sat there. It had been like a security blanket. She always kept it beside her bed when she slept.

She picked it up. It had never been used. Would it work now? She knew the instructions on the can. It would squirt up to twenty feet, more than the length of her living room. She didn't know if it would direct spray or spray upward, but she had to take the chance that this would work. If she used it and missed—

She and Hannah would have to run for their lives. It was as simple as that. Her phone. Where was her phone? She'd used it to call Clare and her mom. It was on the coffee table in the living room.

Hannah was crying now and Beth heard something else hit the floor. She didn't care now if she was quiet. She rushed into the hall and into the living room. In the kitchen, Jed had hold of Hannah's arms. There was only one thing she could do.

She yelled, "Hannah, duck. Hide your face."

Beth saw the moment of understanding in Hannah's eyes. Beth raised the can and sprayed.

As Jed yelled and let go of Hannah, Beth swiped her phone off the coffee table. When Hannah ran to her, Beth grabbed her hand and practically dragged her down the hall. Jed had blocked the door into the kitchen, so they only had one way to go...down the back. She was shaking so badly she could hardly hold onto her phone.

Hannah was asking, "What are we going to do? What are we going to do?"

"We just have to get outside," Beth told her.

"He has a gun."

Oh, my gosh. That changed everything.

They ran down the stairs into the storage room. Beth took a second and brought up Sam's contact number.

She punched in, **9-1-1. He has a gun**.

Up above, she heard Jed rushing down the hall and clomping down the steps after them. She jabbed at the lights in the back of the store. But in their hurry, they bumped into furniture anyway as they ran through it, weaving in and out of dressers and chairs and cupboards with china.

"Stop," Jed yelled behind them. "Or I'll shoot. I swear I'll shoot you both."

Maybe the wasp spray hadn't been a direct hit. She wasn't going to stop running...but Hannah did stop. "Go," her friend said under her breath.

"I'm not leaving you," Beth countered, not caring if Jed heard or not.

Jed was pointing an ugly looking gun at Beth. "So *you're* the one who tried to take her away from me. Who do you think you are?"

"I'm her friend. You hurt her. She deserves better than you."

"Beth..." Hannah warned her.

Beth knew she should be more careful, more tactful, but she was angry, angrier than she'd ever been. She wasn't just angry at Jed. She was angry at any man who would abuse a woman. She was angry at Luther Brown for taking her away from her family, for making her forget who she was.

Beth had been taught many deep breathing exercises over the years. She'd taken yoga and practiced meditation. Right now she called on everything she'd learned to calm herself down, to take a deep breath, to figure out what to do next. *Engage him in conversation*, came an instruction from somewhere. Yes, she'd taken self-defense courses too, but that had been a few years ago and she didn't remember much besides the wasp spray.

Remembering she was in an antique store, she backed up against a highboy. "How did you find us?" she asked conversationally, all temper removed from her tone.

"You can't guess?" he jeered.

"You didn't follow us, we made sure of that."

"This is the tech age, little lady. While you were in that car, sitting outside of Leah's apartment, I put a tracking device on the car under the wheel well. Granted, I didn't know you were in the car at the time, but I knew that tracker would come in handy...and it did. Yeah, you lost me in the streets. I got a little revved up with that chase. But then I just turned on my phone app and followed you to the hotel. The thing was—I wasn't going to get mixed up in hotel security or the local police. So I waited. With the tracker, my phone app was all I needed to find you. I thought about trying to grab Hannah when you made that restaurant stop, but that tall dude was with you. Better to wait for Hannah, or even the two of you, to be alone. That tracker was such a simple thing—just like Hannah coming back with me is going to be a simple thing."

Hannah looked at Beth with pleading eyes. She obviously didn't know what to do. Neither did Beth.

She heard a car outside that sounded like Sam's SUV. But it didn't stop. It mustn't have been him. Maybe she shouldn't have texted him. She didn't want him walking into this. She still had her phone in her hand. All she could do was press 9-1-1 and leave the line open.

She asked Jed, "How do you think you're going to keep Hannah with you if she really wants to run away?"

"She won't run away. She loves me."

Hannah mumbled, "You're delusional."

He lifted the gun and pointed it at her. "What did you say?"

His attention diverted for the moment, Beth glanced down at her phone, changed the screen to her keypad and pressed 9-1-1.

"I said you're delusional." Hannah's voice gained strength and determination. "The first gas station you stop at, the first convenience store, the first time you leave your apartment without me, I'll break out. I'll smash windows. I'll hammer out locks. I won't stay with you."

Beth could hear a voice coming from her phone asking what the emergency was. She said in as loud a voice as she could, "The gun won't do you any good. All you'll do is shoot up the antiques at *Yesteryear's Treasures*."

"Like I care," he yelled back. Jed pointed to the door with his gun and said to Hannah, "Let's go."

"You can't," Beth warned him. "The door's locked and the security system's alarm is on."

Now he pointed the gun at her. "Turn it off."

What Jed didn't know was that there was a panic alarm on the security panel. If she could just hit that and get the door opened, she and Hannah could run out. That's if he was a bad shot.

He wiggled the gun at Beth. "Do what I say."

The voice had stopped coming from the phone and Beth wondered if they were listening or if they'd just hung up thinking this was a crank call.

"I'll turn off the alarm," she said loudly. "Put down the gun."

"Not likely," he said with a bitter laugh.

As Beth moved to the door, she thought she saw a shadow cross in front of the window. Could that be the police? So soon? She was hoping against hope that Clare hadn't arrived.

Approaching the panel, she took her time punching in the code. She told Jed, "I'll have to unlock the door."

"Do it," he commanded. "But don't you set a foot out there. I'm going to lock you in that back storage room."

The idea of *that* gave Beth fresh resolve. She would *never* be locked in a room again. Slowly she unlocked the front door but didn't push it open. Instead she turned slightly then slammed her palm on the panic button on the panel and ducked. A sharp, shrill alarm assaulted her ears.

Jed yelled, "What did you do?"

A gunshot went off and shattered the glass in the door.

Beth felt little shards of glass hitting her, but the bullet missed.

Just then Sam yanked open the door, grabbed her arm and pulled her outside.

"But Hannah's in there."

"I'll get her."

Beth had come to know the store like the back of her hand, and she knew most of what was in it. She caught Sam's arm. "Right inside the door—a fireplace set with a poker."

The alarm was still blaring as Sam slipped inside. Beth wasn't staying outside. She followed him back in and saw him pick up the poker. He kept it down by his side.

Jed had caught Hannah again. He had his arm around her neck in a choke hold.

Sam shouted, "Let her go."

"And just who are you? Her new sugar daddy?"

Beth could see that Hannah was sheer white with fear, and she looked like she was going to pass out. Maybe she couldn't breathe because Jed's arm was so tight against her neck.

"You're choking her," Beth yelled at him. "Let her go."

"Never. No one walks away from me."

Suddenly police sirens sang their unique song in the dark night. Jed's eyes widened and he looked surprised. "That can't be."

"It *can* be, Jed," Sam told him. "Some women are just smarter than you. Beth texted me—**9-1-1. He has a gun.** I knew what that meant. I called 9-1-1. I called the police. They'll be here any second. You're not going to get away, and you'd better loosen your arm from around Hannah's neck or you'll have a murder charge to account for too."

Beth held her breath as Jed looked down at Hannah, slightly loosening his hold. "I loved you," he wailed practically like a child who was told he couldn't have his own way.

Hannah stared at him imploringly. In a whisper she said, "I loved you once, Jed, but then you hurt me. I couldn't stay. You're hurting me now. You don't hurt somebody you love."

The sirens were getting closer.

Sam reminded him, "They'll be here any second. They might even have called in SWAT. Put down the gun."

They could all hear car doors slamming.

Panic shone in Jed's eyes. He looked around—to the side...to the back storage room. He realized he was trapped.

"They'll cover the upstairs outside entrance too," Sam assured him.

"There's got to be a back way out of here," Jed insisted plaintively.

There was, Beth knew. There was a side door that led out of the storage room. It would probably be better if he left that way and let them alone. At least they'd all be safe.

But before she could mention that door, an officer stormed through it! One came in the front at the same time. They had their weapons drawn.

Jed took his arm from around Hannah's neck and flung her away. Then he raised his gun to shoot her.

The officer in blue shot him first.

As Jed fell to the floor, the gun skittered away from him and one of the officers collected it.

Sam called, "I'm a doctor. That's a chest wound. I have to try to keep him alive."

The officer in charge nodded and Sam rushed to Jed. He said to Beth, "I need to put pressure on the wound. Do you have a towel...something?"

Beth didn't hesitate to reach into an armoire drawer and pull out two dresser scarves. She rushed them to Sam. He folded them, used them as padding, and pressed them to Jed's wound. She'd had no medical training but Hannah's ex-boyfriend's injury looked lethal. His face was ashen and blood was everywhere. So much blood. Beth knew she'd never forget the sight of it or the sight of Sam's shirt and hands stained with it.

Two officers escorted Beth and Hannah outside and separated them. It seemed like forever, even though it might have only been five minutes, until the paramedics arrived and an ambulance. Ten minutes later on a gurney with an oxygen cannula in his nose and IVs snaking from his hands, Jed was taken away.

When Sam exited *Yesteryear* another officer separated him to take his statement. He and Beth locked glances and he shook his head. "He lost a lot of blood," he said. "I don't know if he's going to make it."

Clare arrived before Beth finished her statement to the police. Hannah's statement was taking much longer because she had a whole story to tell. Clare must have phoned Max and Amanda because they appeared too. Beth ran to them, hugging them both.

As Max rubbed her back, he said, "Your mother told me about your call earlier. Clare phoned us as soon as she got here. My God, Beth, what happened?"

She ran through it all again but quickly because she wanted to be with Sam. She had to see him and talk to him as soon as she could. He was with a police officer now up on the deck outside her apartment where they'd taken him for his statement. He looked as if he'd been through a war. Maybe they all had.

"I'm not sure which one of you to advise," Max said. "Did any of you touch the gun?"

"No," Beth assured him. "I tried to spray Jed with the wasp spray but I guess I mostly missed because he came after us. If I'd gotten his face, maybe he'd still be alive."

"You can't second-guess a situation like this."

"Sam tried to save his life."

"He did?" Amanda asked as if she might be surprised by that. "That man tried to hurt you and Hannah. Why would Sam do that?"

"Because that's the kind of man Sam is," Beth said softly. She looked up at her father. "Dad, you don't have an extra shirt in your car or something, do you? Sam's going to have to get washed up."

"Actually I have my gym duffel in there. I'm sure I have a T-shirt and jeans. This whole place is going to be considered a crime scene. As soon as you can all leave, we'll go back to our house, then you can all start processing what happened."

Could they start processing it all? Or would it be in their memory banks for as long as they could remember?

The police finally finished with their questions for Hannah. She, Beth and Sam would all have to go down to the station tomorrow and sign statements.

Sam finally came down the steps from the landing. The police officers allowed him to wash up at the spigot in the back. But when he came to the front curb, his shirt was still blood-splattered.

He held out his hands when Beth came toward him to hug him. "I don't want to get this all over you, and not just for cleaning reasons. We don't know what was in his blood." She could see he was just trying to protect her. She could see he meant it.

"Take off your shirt," she said. "I have to touch you."

"Beth."

She stood her ground and didn't move. Max went and got his duffel bag and pulled out the T-shirt. He brought it to Sam. "If she's anything like her mother, she can be damn stubborn."

Sam removed his shirt quickly, wadded it into a ball, and dropped it on the ground. But one of the techs who'd come out of the shop to fetch something in the forensics van, saw it and bagged it.

"We know you didn't shoot him," an officer still standing at the curb said. "But it's evidence."

After a nod, Sam dragged Max's T-shirt over his head. Once he did, Beth wrapped her arms around him. She held on until a little of the tension left his body...until he leaned into her and admitted, "I have to go to the hospital to see how he's doing. I worked on him. I feel it's my responsibility."

"I understand. I'll go with you. I need a minute to talk to Hannah."

He nodded that he'd wait.

Beth went to Hannah and pulled her aside. Then she hugged her tight. When she finally leaned back, she asked, "How are you?"

"I feel numb," she said a little hoarsely. "I can't believe what happened. I once loved him, Beth. At least, I thought I did. I can't believe he came after us like that...like a crazy person."

"He hit you. He hurt you."

"I know. And I knew I had to get away. But part of me...still cares." Her voice broke with emotion.

"I know," Beth assured her. "Sam and I are going to the hospital. But I'm not sure *you* should."

No sooner were the words out of her mouth when Amanda came over to them. "I'm so sorry for what you've been through." Amanda put an arm around each of their shoulders.

Beth quickly introduced the two women. Then her gaze connected with Amanda's. "I don't think Hannah should be alone. Sam and I are going to drive to the hospital." She looked at Hannah. "Mind staying with Amanda and Max?"

Hannah immediately protested. "I don't want to be a bother."

As soon as the words were out of Hannah's mouth, Amanda immediately assured her, "You're *not* going to be a bother. And you can't stay at Beth's apartment because it's considered a crime scene. If you come home with me, I'll make sure you get a warm bath, tea, maybe an omelet or pancakes or both. And you can talk or not talk or whatever you'd like."

When Clare came up behind Amanda, she assured Hannah, "Mom likes taking care of people. And so does Dad. Believe me, if she can cluck over you and cook for you, she'll be happy."

Out of the corner of her eye, Beth saw Sam beckon to her. "I have to go." She studied Hannah. "Will you be okay with Mom?"

Amanda did a double-take because Beth used the title again so naturally. Beth suddenly realized how right the word felt. She'd truly meant it when she'd said it.

Amanda's eyes suddenly flooded with tears, and Beth

knew what the title meant to her. Her own eyes grew teary and she knew she couldn't start crying now or she wouldn't stop crying for a long time. Turning toward her mother, she gave Amanda a hug and kissed her on the cheek.

Hannah said, "You go. I'll be in good hands."

Beth gave her mom's hand a squeeze and a meaningful nod to Clare, then rushed toward Sam and whatever they had to face next.

After they were in the car, Sam turned to her. He said, "I died a thousand deaths after that text you sent me. I didn't know if my barging in would hurt you, if I could save you, if either you or Hannah were already hurt. I can't talk about it now. I have to see if Jed is still alive, then I need to make some calls. But after that, probably very late tonight, I need alone time with you. If Hannah is staying with your mom and dad, maybe you can come to my place. Will you?"

"Yes. I have to talk to you too. Memories came back during everything. I want to sort them out with you."

Sam reached over and took her hand and squeezed it. Then he started the ignition, pulled away from the curb, and stared at the road ahead.

Chapter Eighteen

At the York Hospital, Beth sat outside the ICU in a waiting room. They'd been in the hospital for over an hour now and Sam had been in and out, talking to colleagues. Eventually he stood in the door of the waiting room, his face more stoic than she'd ever seen it.

"How is he?"

"He didn't make it."

"Sam, I'm sorry. At least I'm sorry for you. The truth is, I don't know if I'm sorry for Hannah. Would he ever have left her alone, even from prison?"

Quickly, Sam crossed to her and dropped into a chair beside her. Then he wrapped his arm around her. "I understand how you feel."

"But you tried to save his life."

"I did it because it was the right thing for me to do."

Wearing blue scrubs now so he could navigate the areas of the hospital where he had to go, Sam looked like the physician he was. She remembered when he'd been dressed in blue scrubs before her surgery. She'd liked the look then and she liked the look now.

"You didn't do it just because it was the right thing to do," she countered. "You did it because you save lives. No matter what he did, you had to help. And with everything that happened tonight, don't you see now that you could never be like your father? Don't you see now that you're a good man who would protect the people you love?"

Sam's silence worried her because she wondered if he *did* know that.

Sounding as serious as she'd ever heard him, he said, "I have something to ask you, Beth, but this isn't the kind of place I ever imagined asking you."

She didn't know whether to be afraid or excited. "What do you want to ask me? We're alone. It's quiet in here." Then deciding to relieve some of the worry on his face, she took a plunge and told him exactly what *she* was thinking. "I believe we belong together."

"I see," he murmured.

"Don't *you* believe we belong together?"

"You mean not separated by continents?"

"That's exactly what I mean."

"I made some calls."

At the same time he said that, she said, "I'll go with you to Africa."

They stared at each other. He turned his chair to face hers and gazed straight into her eyes. "I love you. I want to marry you, and I want to marry you soon."

She felt as if all the air had been knocked out of her. She felt as if she were on the verge of her life changing forever.

He went on, "And, of course, I don't want to go to Africa as soon as we're married. That wouldn't be fair to either of us. But neither would *not* getting married and living apart."

"But you signed up for the trip."

"Yes, I did. But that's what my phone calls were about. I have a friend in England who's a plastic surgeon too. I took classes with him when he came here to study. He's as expert a plastic surgeon as I am. He said he'll take my place for Africa. He doesn't have any responsibilities at home—no wife, no kids, no girl friend. He says it's perfect timing."

"Sam, you love that kind of work." Wouldn't he resent her eventually if he sacrificed his work for her?

"Yes, I do love the work. There's an opportunity to go on a shorter trip to Paraguay in late June. We would be in the city of Asuncion. The time frame would be limited to a two week period. Would you consider going along with me on that trip? Paraguay is pretty primitive but I heard there are beautiful sights. We could explore it together."

She considered everything he'd said—*I love you. I want to marry you.* Most of all she thought about a life with him, a family with him, and children.

As if he thought she wouldn't say yes, he took her by the shoulders. "I love you, Beth," he said again. "Tonight I thought I was going to lose you. We need every precious moment we can grasp together. Don't you see that?"

She couldn't make him wait a moment longer. "I *do* see that. And, Sam, I *do* love you. You're mostly what I thought about tonight when I didn't know if I was going to come out of it alive, or I didn't know if *you* were going to survive it because I brought you into danger. I want to make promises to you I will keep for a lifetime. I want to spend every day and every night with you. I want to help in your work if you'll let me. I think two weeks in Paraguay would be a good way to start."

He was smiling now. "Did I hear in there somewhere that you love me?"

"I'll say it as often as you want to hear it. I love you, Sam Benedict, and I believe if we make a wedding promise, we'll keep it."

When Sam kissed her, she knew that kiss was a promise in itself. It was a promise they would nurture for the rest of their lives.

Epilogue

In the small dressing room at the Pine Hill Church where Amanda had gotten remarried, Beth marveled at the fact that six women could pull together a wedding in a month. Her two moms, as she thought of them, Clare, Shara, and Hannah had helped her choose a wedding gown from the shop where Amanda had found hers. Beth had let them decide about bridesmaids gowns and they'd chosen flowered dresses all in different styles that suited each one of them. The floral patterns in pink and blue and yellow mixed together beautifully.

Suddenly, Amanda and Irene came up behind Beth on either side. The three of them looked into the mirror together. Beth felt like a princess in her strapless gown of satin, lace and pearls with a white flower fashioned of lace in her hair. Irene had given her the drop pearl earrings. Amanda had gifted her with a pearl necklace.

Amanda's eyes were already misty. "Do you think we'll all cry at the same time?"

Shara lumbered up beside the two women. She was due in a month, but Beth knew she was more than ready to have this baby. Shara warned, "You're all going to be crying from start to finish."

"And not you?" Clare asked as she circled her daughter with her arm.

"I filled my purse with Kleenex."

Hannah hung back a bit as she usually did, obviously unsure she belonged in this mix. But Beth held her hand out to her. "Are you sure you're going to be okay in my apartment while Sam and I take a short honeymoon?"

Hannah answered her question. "I'll be fine in your apartment. It's starting to feel like home and it's handy for me if I need to check inventory or access the office computer."

"You are *just* what I needed," Amanda said to Hannah. "You've taken to the business like you were meant for it. I know it will be in good hands when I want to babysit my great granddaughter."

Hannah was going to be Amanda's office manager and run the business when Amanda couldn't. Working at the marina for so many years, she had the skills for it and Amanda had picked up on that quickly. It was a win-win situation for everyone.

Beth and Sam had decided to drive to a hotel just for honeymooners tucked into the Catskill Mountains. They simply just wanted to be together—not sit in airports, not worry about security, not have lots of other people around them.

Shara rubbed her back. "I brought a cushion along to use at the reception. I don't think I'll be dancing."

Although Amanda and Max had wanted to spring for a fancier reception at a venue in York, Sam and Beth had decided the social hall of the church would be just fine. Sam was having it catered by a company that often oversaw the foundation's parties and fundraisers. They were mixing old with new, simple with more elaborate. She had the feeling that's the way their lives were going to work.

Strains of organ music wafted in from the church. All six women turned and faced the door.

"It's time," Irene said, tears in her eyes too, as she carefully put her arms around Beth and kissed her. "Are you okay?"

"I'm wonderful," Beth assured her.

They all knew about the memories that had crashed back during the crisis with Hannah. They all knew she'd had several sessions with her therapist again. But all was good because as her therapist had pointed out, the healing after all these years had finally really begun.

Amanda opened the door and waited while the others filed out. Then she took Beth's hand in hers. "This is such a wonderful day that I might fall apart."

"We'll all hold each other together," Beth assured her, feeling stronger than she'd ever felt before.

Amanda must have seen that because she gave her daughter a huge hug then went out to join the others.

In the vestibule, Clare handed out their bouquets. Joe, who was one of the groomsmen, held out an arm to each mom then walked the two of them up the aisle. When he returned, Sam's friends, the other groomsmen, each stepped up to Hannah and then Shara. Joe took Clare's arm.

Beth stood in the vestibule alone staring down the long white runner as her bridesmaids and maid of honor processed ahead of her. Her gaze went to Sam who was standing with the minister at the altar.

Suddenly she was flanked by Max on one side and Roger on the other side. Her two dads. Max had agreed she could call him "Pops" and he was cool with that. Somehow Beth managed to hold on to her bouquet of white and peach-colored lilies as she linked arms with them and they started down the aisle.

Max's voice was filled with emotion as he looked down at her and said, "Today I feel like I can finally breathe again, like you're really here with us and someone is going to care for you the way I always wanted to."

All right. She'd felt strong when she'd started out but now tears threatened. On the other side of her, Roger assured her, "This is the happiest day of our lives. I love you, Pumpkin."

His childhood name for her did it. A tear leaked down her cheek. But she didn't care because she expected there were going to be many more.

The walk to the altar seemed like a dream. But then her two dads stepped away, each kissing her on her cheeks. After she handed her bouquet to Clare and stepped up to the altar with Sam, she faced the reality she was looking forward to for the rest of her life.

Sam wrapped his arm around her whether he was supposed to or not and leaned close. "You are beautiful."

She felt beautiful in a way she never had before. Yet it was the look in Sam's eyes, not the bridal gown, that made her *feel* beautiful.

The minister spoke to friends and family gathered there and then began the ceremony. When they came to the vows, she and Sam faced each other. They had written their own and they were ready to share them.

After a nod from the reverend, Sam began, "I, Samuel Alexander Benedict, take you Beth Lynn Thaddeus Crandall to be my life partner, my best friend, my helpmate, my confidante, and my wife. I don't think I realized who I was until I met you." His voice became deeper and huskier. "You've brought love, honesty, and compassion into my life. You've become my sunshine each day, my solace at night, and most of all, you've become my home. My wedding promise to you is threefold. I promise to be faithful. I promise to give your concerns and needs the same importance as my own. I promise to love and cherish you forever. No matter what life throws at us, I know we can handle it together. I will be yours and you'll be mine until the end of time."

When the minister looked at her to give her the start-ing signal, Beth didn't know if she could speak. Her throat was closed with so much emotion. But her heart was open wide and that's where her courage came from. She squeezed Sam's hands as she gazed into his eyes. "I'm sure my moms and dads always hoped I'd marry a doctor."

There was a slight titter of laughter from the guests gathered in the church.

She went on, "But you're so much more than a doctor. From the moment I met you, I knew compassion was as important to you as your skill. I realized gentleness was part of your character along with your strength. I thought

I was living before I met you, but I'd really wrapped myself in a safe cocoon, and I wasn't enjoying the fullness of my life. Now I feel like a butterfly who is finally free. You showed me how easy it was to be vulnerable again. You showed me how to open my heart to new experiences and most of all, to you. Your understanding and love has brought me here today. My wedding promise to you is also threefold. I will be loyal and true. I will stand by your side whether the stars fall from the sky or whether they shine brightly on us. I will love you with all of my heart from this day forward until our love is the only energy that surrounds who we leave behind. You are my future, Sam Benedict, and I am yours. I vow to treat each day as an adventure and to love you with everything I am."

They held on tightly to each other as they turned to face the minister once more.

The reverend took the rings Clare handed him. He focused on Sam and handed him the ring. "Repeat after me." Sam easily remembered the reverend's words as he pushed the ring onto Beth's finger and said, "With this ring, I thee wed. The circle of gold is a symbol of my love, honor, and protection."

Beth took the ring the minister handed her and she pushed it onto Sam's finger. "With this ring, I thee wed. The circle of gold is a symbol of my love, honor, and protection."

The minister grinned at them. "I now pronounce you husband and wife. Sam, you may kiss your new wife. Beth, you may kiss your new husband."

Sam's arms wrapped around her and they took advantage of the few moments they had to do just that.

Applause broke out and, smiling, they turned to face family and friends. Clare handed Beth her bouquet and with her arm enjoined with Sam's, they walked down the aisle to their future.

About the Author

Award-winning author Karen Rose Smith was born in Pennsylvania. Although she was an only child, she remembers the bonds of an extended family. Since her father came from a family of ten and her mother, a family of seven, there were always aunts, uncles and cousins visiting on weekends. Family is a strong theme in her books and she suspects her childhood memories are the reason.

In college, Karen began writing poetry and also met her husband to be. They both began married life as teachers, but when their son was born, Karen decided to try her hand at a home-decorating business. She returned to teaching for a while but changes in her life led her to writing romance fiction. Now she writes romances and mysteries full time.

Presently, she is hard at work on two mystery series—her Caprice De Luca Home Staging series as well as her Daisy's Tea Garden mysteries. When she isn't writing, she cares for her four rescued cats and assorted strays, cooks, gardens and photographs all. She enjoys interacting with her readers on social media.

Married to her college sweetheart since 1971, believing in the power of love and commitment, she envisions herself writing relationship novels, both romance and mystery, for a long time to come!

KAREN ROSE SMITH BOOKS
AVAILABLE IN E-BOOK FORMAT

FINDING MR. RIGHT Series
Kit and Kisses, Book 1 *
Forever After, Book 2 *
When Mom Meets Dad, Book 3 *
Falling For Her Boss, Book 4 *
Toys and Baby Wishes, Book 5 *
Love in Bloom, Book 6 *
Ribbons and Rainbows, Book 7 *
Wish on the Moon, Book 8 *
A Man Worth Loving, Book 9 *

SEARCH FOR LOVE Series
Nathan's Vow, Book 1 *
Jake's Bride, Book 2 *
Always Devoted, Book 3 *
Always Her Cowboy, Book 4 *
Heartfire, Book 5 *
Cassidy's Cowboy, Book 6 *
Her Sister, Book 7 *
The Wedding Promise 8 *

EVERYDAY LOVE Short Story Series
Everyday Cinderellas, Vol. 1
Everyday Prince Charming, Vol. 2
Everyday Romance, Vol.3

Garden of Fantasy
Abigail and Mistletoe
Writing is a Business

SCIENCE FICTION
SHORT STORY COLLECTION
Journey Into Chaos

BOXED SETS
Finding Mr. Right Box Set One
Finding Mr. Right Boxed Set Two
Search For Love Boxed Set One
Search For Love Boxed Set Two
Everyday Love Boxed Set

*Also available as an audio book

Prologue

D*on't answer it.*
Don't answer it.
*Do **not** answer it.*

Gillian Moore convinced herself to ignore the intrusive sound of the ringing telephone as the golden L.A. sun swept through her open living room window, along with the balmy June breeze.

Her phone rang a second time.

Plucking the leatherbound volumes from her bookshelf one by one, she dusted them with a soft cloth. She always cleaned and straightened her surroundings when her heart or mind was in turmoil. With a quick glance at the phone on her end table, she knew her mother wouldn't be calling on a Monday evening. Madge Moore called her daughter from Deep River, Indiana every Sunday at exactly seven p.m.

Gillian's phone rang a third time.

She swiped the cloth across the shelf, back and forth.

In the three months since she'd relocated to L.A., she hadn't confided in anyone or encouraged close friendships. She needed this respite. She needed to find out whether her "gift" would continue to be the major force in her life or whether she had a right to keep it in the background, maybe even completely under wraps.

Her phone rang a fourth time.

It could only be **him**—the man who had called the past two nights, the man with the compelling voice, tinged with authority, commanding in its intensity as it directed her to return his call. She didn't know what he wanted, but she could guess. Heaven knew how he'd gotten her number because no one in L.A. had it, not even the manager where she worked.

Her answering machine kicked on with her brief direction for the caller to leave a message. Her usually lilting tone was serious and cool. She ran her hand through her long, light brown hair. Maybe she should get it cut short…make yet another change in her life. She'd made so many in moving here—she actually had time to herself…to be out in the sun, ride a bike, take long walks. She'd found peace along with the bright California sun and she wasn't ready to let go of either.

"Ms. Moore. This is Nathan Bradley. Again," he added in a deep, almost censuring baritone. "In case you haven't received my earlier messages, I need to speak with you immediately about a matter of great urgency." He paused. "Ms. Moore, I *must* speak with you. Please return my call." He gave his number slowly, hesitated a moment, then clicked off.

Gillian stopped dusting. He hadn't said "please" in his

other messages. This time there was a quiet desperation in his tone. She recognized the emotion because the people she'd helped in the past had all been desperate. Nathan Bradley didn't sound like a man who was accustomed to using the word "please," and the huskiness edging the word made her feel vulnerable and guilty, two of the burdens from which she'd tried to escape.

Now this man had brought them to the surface once more. She *wouldn't* return his call. She deserved unpressured time to think about the direction of her life, to have fun working at something she'd never imagined she'd enjoy. Nathan Bradley could find someone else to solve his problem, someone else with a "gift" that had begun to feel more like a curse.

Chapter One

Nathan didn't want to be caught dead, let alone alive, inside a beauty salon. As he pulled open the glass door and stepped inside, feminine chatter, strange smells, and the glimpse of a woman with her hair rolled in blue and purple curlers was enough to make him decide he'd rather face ten irate CEO's whose firewalls had been breached in one day than to plow into this women's domain. But he'd do anything to find his daughters.

Anything.

Nathan's determination had pulled him out of the poverty of his childhood, earned him a scholarship to college, and pushed him to start his own company specializing in computer security after only a year with another firm. He'd wanted to be his own boss, bill his own hours, set his own standards. His determination couldn't save his marriage, but by God, it would lead him to his daughters. After six months of dead ends, he'd decided money and rational strategies weren't enough. That's why he was here. That's why he had to speak to Gillian Moore.

At his private investigator's insistence, Nathan had agreed to go this route—the only route left as far as Nathan was concerned or he wouldn't pursue it. He wouldn't debate about methods, not even weird ones at this point. He'd used every skill he'd possessed to find his daughters. So had his P.I. Now he had to put his logic and wariness aside if he hoped to find his children before he lost more time with them.

The woman at the desk inside the door smiled as her gaze traveled from his dark brown hair, down his charcoal pinstripe suit and striped silk tie, to his black winged-tip shoes. She tilted her head and her lips curved up a bit more. "Can I help you?"

Suddenly Nathan felt as if he were the center of attention. Two customers on chairs in the room beyond had craned their necks to avidly assess him along with the receptionist. His shirt collar felt tighter, and he resisted the urge to tug down his tie. "I'm looking for Gillian Moore."

"You want a manicure?" the redheaded, perfectly coiffed and made-up receptionist asked with a mischievous smile.

"No. My name is Nathan Bradley. I need to speak with her as soon as possible," he said in his best authoritarian tone. "Is she here?"

"Hold on a sec," the redhead answered, her smile flagging. Disappearing into the room beyond, she reappeared a few moments later. "She's with a client. She says she'll talk to you in five minutes."

Five minutes. What the heck was he supposed to do for five minutes? He spied several magazines in a basket in the corner beside two director's chairs. "Fine. I'll wait."

Waiting wasn't something Nathan did well. He hadn't become a successful CEO with company locations across the country by waiting. As he flipped one glossy page after the other, he was vaguely aware this publication didn't advertise fast cars or designer clothes. Tuning in to the sound of feminine voices in the next room, he tried to pick out the one belonging to a woman who had helped police departments solve missing person cases. As he had many times in the past few days, he imagined what she might look like. Probably fuzzy, wild hair with a red scarf tied around her head.

He could feel the receptionist watching him as she pretended to study the schedule book. Finally, a customer with bright crimson nails emerged from the room beyond and gingerly opened her purse at the desk.

"Gillian can see you now," the desk-keeper informed him.

Gillian Moore's lack of response to his phone calls had irritated and frustrated Nathan. He was accustomed to being in charge. But his reason for being here brushed all that aside.

Striding into the busy room, he took it in with one glance—the chairs, mirrors, blow dryers, three hairdressers chatting to their customers. But then his gaze fell on the small white wrought-iron desk in the far corner and the woman sitting behind it. Her face turned away from him, she slid a pack of acrylic nails to the side of the glass top and straightened her manicure paraphernalia. At his approach, her gaze met his, and he almost stopped short.

She didn't look like a psychic.

Her long, light brown hair was laced with sunny

blond highlights. A few tendrils wisped along her cheek. Her bangs wafted across her honey brows. But it was her huge brown eyes that almost immobilized him. They didn't appraise him physically...they looked into his soul. He didn't like the invasion.

Gillian had wished her client a good day and unnecessarily organized her work table, hoping Nathan Bradley had decided not to wait. When she turned her head and saw a tall man with resolve shouting from his furrowed dark brows, the set of his mouth, and his slightly squared jaw, she realized it would take more than a few unanswered phone messages to deter this man.

Taking a slow breath and maintaining eye contact, she slid her hands into the pockets of her white apron. Nathan Bradley wanted something from her, all right, and she couldn't give it. Not right now.

"Ms. Moore."

It was more statement than question. She nodded.

"Could we talk for a few minutes?"

She gestured to her desk. "I'm working, Mr. Bradley. I really don't have time—"

"You don't have a client at the moment," he countered, his blue eyes steady, his voice firm.

This man could be intimidating. But she was used to dealing with hard-nosed cops, jaded private investigators, and a disbelieving public who wanted her help anyway. "No, I don't. But I am working. Now, if you'd like a manicure..." She almost had to smile at his expression of distaste, but then his next words made her heart beat faster.

"I want a few minutes with you. You're the last option I have."

"For what?" she asked, though she sensed what he needed.

"My two daughters. I need you to help me find them."

As she stood, Gillian glanced around the shop to make sure no one was listening. "Where did you get my name?"

"Does it matter?" As he asked, he slipped a photo from the inside pocket of his jacket.

His movement was quick, but Gillian caught a view of a narrow waist, slim hips, and a physique probably as taut as his demeanor and voice. When he offered her the photograph, her attention returned to the situation at hand and she took a step back.

The two young girls in the snapshot had their father's blue eyes and brown hair. She could tell that he loved them from the way the camera had caught Nathan Bradley' expression as he crouched down between them, one arm around each daughter. The pain in his eyes now attested to the fact.

He tried to hand Gillian the photo, but she wouldn't take it. She knew what might happen if she did. She might see images and feel emotions she didn't want right now. Folding her hands in front of her, she said, "I'm no longer doing that type of work."

But it was difficult for her to tear her gaze from the picture. When she did, the sadness in Nathan Bradley's eyes was almost as difficult to ignore.

"Why?"

For some reason, she couldn't hedge or lie to this man. Checking again to be sure no one eavesdropped,

Gillian lowered her voice anyway. "Since I was sixteen, Mr. Bradley, my life hasn't been my own. I came to L.A. to escape the type of work you want me to do and to make decisions about my future." She stopped and tears pricked her eyes as she thought about the last few months before leaving Indiana.

Regaining her composure, she swallowed and went on, "For almost ten years, I've helped others when they've asked. Now I need time and breathing room before I decide if and how I want to use my gift again."

As she spoke, she could tell he listened. There was a spark of empathy in his eyes, but, of course, his need was more important. "Take this one case," he insisted. "I'll protect your privacy if that's what you're concerned about. Your help doesn't have to be public knowledge. I'm an internet security specialist. I know what safeguards we can take. No one else has to know you're here."

She steeled herself against the man's masculine appeal and turned away from the wonderful smiles of the children in the photo as well as the hurt still lingering in her heart. That hurt sprang up every time she remembered Brian Reston and the search for his son, the months she'd dreamed about a future for the three of them.

Despite the time that had passed, despite the miles between L.A. and Deep River, Indiana, she knew she wasn't ready for Nathan Bradley and his search...for any of it. The general public thought psychics could "know" anything they wanted, that they could answer any question, even their own personal ones. That just wasn't true. Gillian had realized early on that she couldn't use her "gift" for her own benefit or to predict events. All she could do was tune into impressions and use them along with her intuition. Words, pictures, and sounds sometimes popped into her head, but she never knew when that was going to happen. It hadn't happened since she'd left Indiana.

With the need for self-preservation being her overriding concern, she said, "If you found me, others will be able to. And I'm not only concerned about privacy. You make my help seem simple, as if all I have to do is close my eyes and give you the answers you want. The process is much more complicated than that. Try a private investigator, Mr. Bradley. It will be best for both of us."

"A private investigator gave me your name."

She sighed and shook her head. "Then he can find someone else who does my kind of work."

"It's difficult to find a reputable psychic," Nathan almost growled as his frustration became evident.

Worry stabbed Gillian. "Sh..." All she needed was her co-workers knowing.

Nathan lifted his hands in exasperation and in a loud whisper asked, "Why is it so all-fired important for no one to know what you do?"

Anger bubbled up inside her because this man knew nothing about the hundreds of letters she received each year, the sleepless nights, the burden of parents and brothers and sisters and children depending on her to find someone they loved, or someone who was missing. What irritated her the most were those who wanted a plan for the future without formulating it themselves. "If they knew what I was able to do, most women in this salon would want a reading. They'd line up for hours waiting with bated breath for me to tell them their future. And if I couldn't tell them anything, they'd say I'm a fraud. My gift creates a three-ring circus, Mr. Bradley. No, thank you."

Harriet came in from the front desk. "A walk-in for nails is waiting, Gillian. How's your schedule?"

Gillian accepted fate's offer of a neat, non-confrontational way to end this encounter. "Tell her to come in. I don't have another appointment until four. If it's all right with you, I'll take my supper break at five."

"No problem." Harriet's interest in Nathan was obvious as she gave him a wink and returned to the front room.

He faced Gillian. "I'd like to continue our discussion."

"There's nothing more to say. I have to get back to work and I'm sure you do, too. Call your P.I. He'll find someone else."

The look the man gave Gillian was not resigned. If anything, it was more determined than ever. But he didn't argue. "I'll call my P.I. But I'll be talking to you again. Soon."

With a lift of his brow and a wave of his hand, he was gone.

Gillian first felt relief, then a strange sense of loss. But she was used to feelings and images not clicking. Eventually they became part of a bigger picture, and then she'd understand. But there was no bigger picture where Nathan Bradley was concerned. There was no picture at all.

The instant Gillian stepped outside of the Hair Happening, she saw him. He stood beside a gray Mercedes in the parking lot. She should have realized this man wouldn't give up so easily. Ducking back into the salon was an option. So was ignoring him as she walked to the enchilada and chili stand across the parking lot of the strip shopping center. But she had the feeling when she returned, he'd still be waiting, and not quite so patiently.

A group of teenagers on roller-blades skated by, one of them holding a miniature schnauzer on a leash. She smiled at the sight, something she'd probably never see in Deep River. But her smile slipped as she spotted the handsome, very sexy man walking toward her, and an excited little shiver zipped up her spine. At least six-two, lean and fit, with long legs that quickly covered the distance between them, he was the type of man who could attract a roomful of women without trying. It wasn't only his looks but his confidence, his dominating male presence.

When he stood before her, he asked, "Can I buy you supper?"

"If I hadn't mentioned my break, you would have waited till I quit for the day. Right?"

"Yes."

"Mr. Bradley..."

"Nathan. You have to eat supper. I have to eat supper. Is there any reason we shouldn't talk while we do?"

"You have an ulterior motive. This won't be much of a break for me."

"It's not an ulterior motive because you know what I want."

"Obviously, I need to watch what I say with you," she murmured.

The corners of his mouth twitched up. "Is that a yes or no?"

"If I say no, you'll be back. Let's get this over with."

The curve of his lips turned into a frown, indicating he was uncomfortable with her frankness. Gillian's gaze wanted to linger on those lips. They were full enough to be sensual, narrow enough to enhance the handsome aesthetics of his face. She could imagine one of his kisses—dominating, forceful, passion-filled.

The image startled her. She hadn't thought about kissing a man in over a year—since Brian had decided to reconcile with his ex-wife. She'd not only lost Brian but his son, too. At the time she'd thought her heart would break. But she'd buried herself in her work until she'd realized she no longer had a life outside of her work. Not eating, not sleeping, working twenty hours a day was a one-way road to disaster. Thank goodness she'd recognized her destructive direction in time.

"I don't know what you have in mind," she said, "but the chili and enchiladas are good at that stand over there."

Nathan perused the truck/restaurant set-up near an island with palm trees and benches. "I haven't had an enchilada in..." He shrugged. "Too long."

They walked side by side for a few moments, Nathan slowing his stride to Gillian's. The breeze ruffled his hair, making him look less formal and imposing. She thought he'd start making his case for her help, but he didn't.

His arm brushed hers, his suitcoat rough against her skin. "Have you always done manicures for a living?"

She registered the texture of the material, the strength of his arm, and her heart jumped at the contact. Managing a smile, she responded, "Would you believe I have a degree in business?"

"Neither seems appropriate for a psychic."

Her smile faded. "And what does? Theater arts?"

He stopped and faced her. "Okay. I stuck my foot in it. I didn't mean to insult you. But all this is strange to me. I'm a logical man. I make decisions and judgments from facts. I've always thought psychics were frauds. But my private investigator told me about crimes you've solved and people you've found. Even if I don't believe in it or understand it, what you do works."

"I don't understand it, either," she said quietly.

Nathan had been fascinated by the woman since he'd set his eyes on her. Looking at her now, her soft, long hair, those wonderful brown eyes, her slender curves wrapped in a pink cullotte dress with a white collar and lapels, his muscles tightened and he felt pangs of arousal.

Crazy. That usually didn't happen simply from looking.

Her soft voice, her calm wonder, urged him to step closer, to find out more about her. "Tell me about it. Were you born with this ability?"

She shook her head and pointed to the supper truck. They began walking again. "I don't think I was born with it. If I was, I didn't know it until I was ten. I was sitting on a dock fishing and a storm came up. The thunder and lightning hit fast. The next thing I knew I was lying flat on the dock, the rain pouring down on me.

My head hurt and I was shaking all over. Mom found me that way, took me home, and put me to bed. We thought that was the end of it."

His P.I. had told Nathan that Gillian was from Indiana and had lived there all her life. She traveled often but had never moved from the town where she'd grown up. L.A. must be quite a change for her. "When did you realize something was different?"

"A few days later. Aunt Flora came to visit. When she hugged me, I saw this picture of her sitting at her kitchen table crying. I didn't understand it. Later, I overheard my aunt and my mother talking. My cousin had dropped out of high school and my aunt was terribly upset."

"And there was no way you could have known that."

"No."

"Did you tell your mom?"

"No. I was afraid of the pictures when they came and uncomfortable with the feelings. I kept it a secret until I was sixteen."

They reached the vending stand. Gillian ordered chili and cornbread while Nathan asked for an enchilada. She opened her purse, but he closed his hand over hers. Her skin was soft and warm and a jolt of desire more powerful than before stabbed him. "I've got it," he said, unable to keep the husky rasp from his voice.

Her gaze met his. The sparks of gold in the brown told him his touch affected her as much as hers affected him. She pulled away, and he let go.

Gillian busied herself pulling napkins from the holder while Nathan paid for and carried their plates to a bench. Picking up their sodas, she joined him. She'd no sooner settled on the bench with her soda by her shoe and the cup of chili with a wedge of cornbread perched on the edge in her hand when the schnauzer she'd seen earlier ran over to her and jumped up and down, finally landing with her paws on Gillian's knees.

Gillian laughed and held her dish a little higher, out of the dog's reach. "You might want supper, but I'm not sure you should have this."

One of the roller-bladers came skating over, his helmet under his arm, a leash dangling from his hand. "Sorry if she's botherin' you. She begs from everybody."

The boy was about twelve. His spiked brown hair was matted down from his helmet, his snapping brown eyes sparkled with amusement. Gillian asked him, "Can she have a bite?"

He grinned. "If you wanna give it to her."

Gillian tried to tear off a piece of the cornbread, but it slid into the chili. Nathan grabbed the dish and held it for her. Smiling her thanks, she took the small bite from the wedge and let the dog lick it from her hand. The schnauzer gulped it down and looked up at her for more. Laughing again, Gillian scratched the pet behind her ears. "I should have known that little bit wouldn't be enough."

As she touched the dog and rubbed her rough coat, Gillian felt her gaze pulled to the teenager again. He and the dog were connected by a strong bond of affection. A surge of energy made her fingers tingle and she automatically closed her eyes for a moment. A clear picture of a dark-haired woman on a porch came into focus. The woman was worried. Gillian had the distinct impression she was the boy's mother.

Opening her eyes, Gillian cast a wary look at Nathan. He was watching her closely. Should she say something to the boy about his mother? If she did, Nathan would know what had happened. Why had this vision come now? Since she'd left Indiana, she'd felt normal—no pictures, no knowledge she shouldn't have.

Gillian looked at the boy, knowing she couldn't let the woman in her mind's eye suffer unnecessarily. "I think your dog wants a full-course meal."

"What time is it?" he asked with a nod at Gillian's watch.

"Five-thirty."

"Geez. I was supposed to be home an hour ago. Mom's gonna be..." He stopped with a shrug as if a boy his age shouldn't worry about adult authority. Snapping the leash onto the dog's collar, he gave it a gentle tug. "C'mon, Peanut. We'll get us both some supper." He smiled at Gillian and skated over to his friends, who sat on the curb sipping sodas.

Nathan handed Gillian her plate. "What happened?"

"You saw what happened. I gave the dog a snack."

"When you touched the dog, you closed your eyes."

The man was too observant. "The boy's mother was worried about him."

"You felt that?"

"I saw that. She was standing on the porch waiting for him."

"You got that from petting the dog?" Nathan asked, astonished.

She'd faced expressions like his many times in the past. "Mr. Bradley..."

"Nathan," he reminded her.

Calling him by his first name seemed too familiar. She already knew she could be attracted to him. "This 'talent' I have isn't something I can turn off and on like a light switch. It's more unpredictable than the weather or earthquakes."

"You made him realize she was worried without saying it, without telling him you knew."

"That was easiest."

Nathan finished his enchilada and took a swig of soda before he spoke again. "My ex-wife took my daughters out of the country six months ago. I can't find them. My P.I. can't find them. Will you take my case?"

www.ingramcontent.com/pod-product-compliance
Lightning Source LLC
Chambersburg PA
CBHW021950170626
46808CB00001B/94